The Phantom Letters

A Phantom Heart Series Book 2

By Sarah Wilkins

This book, as well as the book before it, is dedicated to the actor Gerard Butler, whose portrayal as The Phantom in the 2004 film was my main inspiration for these stories.

I also dedicate this book to my readers. Without your support and feedback I could not have done this. Thank you!

Story One: The Phantom Letters

Chapter 1: Just A Joke?

A/N: Readers, I bid you welcome to the corners of my mind. Please join me in exploring my imagination, as this is a story genre I have not written in before. You will be completely submerged into the mind of Erik, AKA Opera Ghost, AKA the Phantom of the Opera. Please, take a seat, relax, and enjoy this story. As always, I do not own Phantom of the Opera or any of its characters.

Erik cursed under his breath as he made his way down the passageway toward the dressing room. Surely Meg knew by now that when Christine was in the chapel, she needed time to be alone! To make matters worse, Christine had actually told Meg about him, and now the little dancer was actually trying to turn his pupil against him!

As if he didn't have enough on his mind. Just this afternoon he had found yet another one of the anonymous notes addressed to him, congratulating him on removing Carlotta from the premises. It was not the first letter, and he had no doubt that it was not the last, either. It would drive any normal person insane. But no, he was the Phantom of the Opera, and no one would be allowed to crawl under his skin, especially one who hides behind letters.

As he stormed through the passageways, he thought back to the first note three years ago. It had been a single line. Three if you counted the greeting and the signing. But it had been enough to amuse him at best.

"Dear O.G.,

I thought I should let you know that you have an admirer in the opera house.

Sincerely,

Someone"

Admirer, he had scoffed. *Who in their right mind would ever admire me?* It was a joke. It had to be. And so, he had dismissed it as just that. He'd had other things to think about anyway. The manager had hired a new lead soprano, an Italian diva named Carlotta. Although how she ever reached that status was completely beyond him. Why, even her so-called devotees stuffed their ears as soon as she opened her mouth! From the moment he first heard her sing, he vowed to not stop until Carlotta was clear across the world from his aching ears, and Christine was permanently singing in her place.

The idea of the notes being nothing more than a joke, however, was quickly stamped out. Over the past three years, he had found several notes in his passageway, seeming to be slipped through one of the vents. The writer was careful not to act in a set pattern, and so he was always caught off-guard. Oh, how he loathed to admit that! After all, he was the Opera Ghost, and this was his theater!

Erik stopped outside the dressing room mirror, pushing his thoughts aside. Seeing that the coast was clear, he slipped into the dressing room, delivered his gift, and ducked back into the passageway mere seconds before Christine entered with Madame Giry at her side. Just as planned, Antoinette handed the young soprano the red rose with his signature black ribbon tied around the stem. For a moment, he contemplated returning to the caverns. However, Meg's words from mere minutes before echoed in his mind. "Christine you had to be dreaming. Stories like this are impossible!" *No, Meg, I am not a dream. And I'll prove it to her!* Yes, tonight he would show Christine that he was real.

Before he could think of having second thoughts, the young Vicomte de Chagny entered the room, and the look on Christine's eyes caused a bitter taste to enter Erik's mouth. Yet for some strange reason, he felt cemented to the floor, as if some invisible being were forcing him to watch the reunion. The longer their conversation lasted, the more Erik felt rage building up inside him. At last, the Vicomte left, and Erik saw his chance. While Christine was changing, he sneaked around and locked the dressing room door. He could feel a pair of eyes upon him, but he brushed the feeling aside. All he could think about was taking action before he had second thoughts. Making his way back behind the mirror, he waited until Christine was about to leave before using his voice.

    During their lessons over the past ten years, he had learned that anytime he let his anger show, she would be quick to apologize and do things his way. Yes, it was working now, for as he voiced his anger towards Raoul, Christine's response was to all but beg for his forgiveness. Erik smirked. She was right where he wanted her, like a blob of clay in his hands. Slowly, he lit a single candle in the passageway, enough to reveal himself to her, yet little enough that it remained almost dreamlike. The last thing he wanted to do was frighten her and appear all at once. No, she was too precious to him. He began calling her closer, and she slowly followed his command. Vaguely, he could hear the Vicomte trying to open the door, and he made his voice only slightly more urgent. Keeping his eyes locked on her trance-like gaze, he slowly slid the mirror open, extending his black leather-gloved hand through the gap. A good part of him wanted to grab her hand and pull her through, but he forced himself to wait for her to make the next move. Finally, contact was made as she took his hand, and he hesitated for only a minute, closing his eyes and taking a deep breath before proceeding to lead her the long way through the passageways and to the lake where his boat was waiting. The journey was far from awkward and silent, for they sang with each other a duet he had taught her only recently.

Once they reached his caverns, however, his insides began to shake with uneasiness. No one, not even Madame Giry, had ever been here other than himself, and this was far beyond his comfort zone. Christine looked at him, watching his every move, seeming to be waiting for him to say something, anything. Finally, he began singing again, a song that he had always found comforting. Several lines were made up on the spot, allowing him to convey his desire for her to see the beauty of his darkness and his music. Oh, to be sure, she had already discovered the beauty of the latter, but to him, darkness and music went hand-in-hand.

And tonight, singing this song and having Christine in his arms, it felt like a dream, and he was secretly afraid that if he blinked just once, she would disappear. And so he kept his eyes fixed on her as she took in the sight of him and their surroundings. He kept his hands on her, not wanting to ever let go. He had not planned for this. That is, he had not planned on it happening tonight. He had no idea as to where to go from here. And so, when he showed Christine the wedding dress he had made for her, and when she fainted in his arms, he was thankful that he at least knew what to do then. He gently picked her up and carried her to his massive brass bed. Laying her down on the velvet-covered mattress, he stroked her face, not daring to remove his glove and make direct contact. Not yet. Yes, she needed sleep. After all, it had been a long day, between the change in management, her reunion with Raoul, and her debut. *And on top of all that, you bring her down here. What were you thinking?* He walked away from the bed then, cursing his thoughts for doubting him. And yet, they had a point. Sighing, he could only hope that she would think of his actions as nothing more than the beginning of a dream. To enhance the effect, he brought his music box over to the bedside table. He would wind it up in the morning—a soothing tune for her to wake up to.

In the meantime, he needed space. Having guests was foreign enough, but this was Christine. *Christine!* He didn't trust himself to stick around any longer than he had to. She was safe, and that was good enough for him. Getting into the boat, he decided a long stroll through the passageways was exactly what he needed. It had always been his 'Plan B' when he was in need of inspiration, but then, on these strolls, he could always count on seeing Christine. Gritting his teeth at the thought, he hoped that he would able to come up with the plan he needed anyway.

The last thing he wanted or needed or planned on was to find another note. But there it was, under the usual vent. *Two in one day?* Had that happened in the past, he certainly would have ignored it and continued with his stroll. But the fact was, it hadn't happened. Letting an exasperated sigh escape his throat, he bent over and picked the envelope up. He was too exhausted and frustrated to bother with being careful as he ripped it open.

"Dear Phantom,

You have a wonderful voice. It would do wonders for the stage. Do consider it. And please be careful with Christine. You are not the only one who finds her precious.

Sincerely,

Someone"

I was right. I didn't need to hear that! Me, on the stage? Who do they think I am? His hands began shaking uncontrollably, whether from pure rage or nervousness, he couldn't tell. Whoever this was, they were getting too close. Way too close. He glanced back down at the note to see if there were any clues hidden in the message, but to his dismay, he realized he had torn it to shreds. For the millionth time since he had gotten the first note, he peered through the vent. Just as before, it provided no help, as the room appeared to be accessible to everyone in the opera house.

But wait...me on stage...yes, it just might work... The inspiration he had been looking for hit him just then, and he raced back to the caverns. He needed to write, and morning would be soon upon them.

Chapter 2: Phantom Tears and Phantom Fears

"And...you were the man inside the boat..." Startled, Erik turned from his music to face the source of the voice. Christine. Yes, he had only minutes before wound up the music box for her, but he had immediately returned to the song he'd been working on all night, and as soon as his pen touched the paper, he'd gotten lost all over again. Only Christine, with that beautiful voice that he had crafted, could have brought him back to reality. And yet, even as she began to approach him, he could not stop working. Turning back to the organ, he began testing the notes out, caught in the sway of the music. He felt her moving closer still, and he felt her hand on his face long before the contact was made. *Finally... this is how I imagined it... this can be our future...* Just then, however, he felt a sudden draft on the right side of his face. And that could only mean one thing. Enraged and ashamed, he flung her to the cushioned stone bench and brought his hand swiftly to his face. No! How could she! It wasn't as if he planned on deceiving her forever. He was just waiting for the best moment...a moment where she would be comfortable enough in his presence...

But no. Her impatience and curiosity had gotten the best of her, and now there was nothing left to hide behind. "Curse you!" Somehow, he had to salvage this. He had seen the look of complete horror on her face, and he had to show her that he was more than a monster. Everything he had put his heart and soul into the past several years depended on it. He knew that she already had it in her to see into his soul. All those nights singing to her, speaking to her...there was no way around it. She just needed to listen to him again...yes, he could fix this. And so, using his words and his music, he pleaded with her to look past the repulsiveness of his face, to even look past his 'Opera Ghost' reputation and see that he was a man...a lonely, empty man, but a man nonetheless. Finally, overcome by pent up emotion and tears, he collapsed on the stone steps. "Oh, Christine..."

He heard her stir, but he didn't dare to look. She seemed to be moving towards him, however, and his heart grabbed onto that last shred of hope. *Yes...come to me, my love...take me into your arms...tell me everything will be okay...* Instead, his mask appeared beside him. *That's okay. Forget what you've seen. We'll start over.* He slowly covered his face again, then took a deep breath before standing to help her up. Yes, he would return her now to the upstairs. She would get her much-needed rest, and he would work on continuing her career. Hopefully, when she awakened, she would think of this night as nothing more than a dream.

Erik stopped in his tracks. *No, I just imagined it.* But as he turned to look again, there was no mistaking the square of white for anything but another note. *If this is about Christine, whoever-you-are, you must learn to be patient. I just now returned her to you!* But as he read the message, his emotions changed completely.

"Dear O.G.,

I have a favor to ask of you. There is a certain stagehand by the name of Joseph Buquet. I assume you know of him, as you seem to know everything that happens within these walls. I must ask you to do something about him. He is spreading lies about you for one thing. But he has gotten worse. I fear he will attack one of the many young ladies backstage if he ever gets the chance. Please do something, and I will be eternally grateful.

Sincerely,

Your Admirer."

Joseph Buquet. Oh, Erik knew of him, all right. Ever since the scoundrel had been hired on, Erik had watched him carefully. There had always been something about the man that he didn't like, and soon enough, he had been able to put his finger on it. The drink. Erik was no stranger to the effects the drink can have on one's judgment. Reluctantly, his thoughts went back to his days in the fair. He recalled how his gypsy "master" seemed to be glued to one bottle or another. Only in front of the crowds had he let go of his drink, but Erik figured it was just to free up his hands to grab up the money flung at him through the cage bars. It was the drink that had caused all those beatings, whether in front of the jeering crowds or when it was just the two of them. It had also made it easy for Erik to slip out of his bindings that fateful night and end that man's greedy life. But there was no way, no way, any of the girls would fall victim to a drunken stagehand. Not while he was still Phantom of the Opera!

For once, he did not look for any clues within the note. He would gladly do this favor, a hundred times over. He only wondered why he hadn't taken care of Buquet before. No matter. He had his reason to do it now. Someone was complaining, and he would not let them down. He was thankful that he had just delivered his own stack of notes. Perhaps this could turn into a win-win situation. If everyone obeyed his instructions, then all would be well, and he could quietly dispose of Buquet long after Il Muto was over. And if those foolish managers went against him...Erik smirked at the plan and made his way back down into his caverns.

As he moved through the passageways, he heard a racket of singing voices which he could not ignore, coming from the other side of the wall. One belonged to that talentless diva, and he cringed. *So, they prefer her over Christine, do they? They don't take orders? We shall see, gentlemen. We shall see.*

That night, Erik moved quickly to put his plan into play. As he switched Carlotta's precious spray bottle for his own special concoction, he again felt a pair of eyes upon him. He did not have time for guessing games, however. He needed to move fast if he was going to snatch the first opportune moment. As he passed over the stage, he glared down at Christine's replacement, as if he could burn a hole through the stage beneath her. *She'll be humbled soon enough, Erik. Keep moving.* He made his way to the top of the dome, where his voice would have maximum effect. At the first pause in the song below, he spoke, keeping his voice at his normal volume, but unmistakably clear. The echo did the rest of the work. "Were you not told to keep Box Five empty?" The music halted immediately, and he could hear several gasps from below him. Thankfully, he had positioned himself so no one would be able to see him. Smirking, he watched Carlotta go offstage to get a dose of the spray, just as he had predicted. The smirk stayed on his face as he went back through the door. Carlotta's inevitable humiliation would provide sufficient distraction while he acted out the second half of his plan.

Yes, everything was working perfectly. *Buquet, you foolish man. Have you not heard that curiosity killed the cat? This stagehand has no idea what he's getting himself into.* In no time at all, the tables were turned, and now it was Erik chasing Buquet. The stagehand had been drinking again, not surprisingly, and so it was easy for Erik to herd him onto one of the wooden bridges. Laughing inside, the Phantom grasped the ropes holding the bridge in place, and he shook it just until Buquet lost his footing. Moving effortlessly, Erik brought out his lasso and forced it over the drunk's head. As he pulled the rope tighter and tighter, he bent down and whispered in his victim's ear. "This is for any of those innocent young ladies you've offended. May you drink not one more drop on this Earth!" With that, he looped the other end of the rope over one of the dangling hooks, then shoved Buquet over the edge of the bridge and out of his sight. He lingered only for a moment, watching the dancers on stage react. You're welcome, he wished he could say. The rope soon came undone from the hook, but the deed had been done.

With a swish of his cape, Erik made his way up to the rooftop, his second sanctuary. He needed air...fresh air. Only when he had crouched behind one of the massive statues did his hands begin to shake. He did not have time to think about what he had just done, however, for he heard someone burst through the rooftop door. "The Phantom of the Opera doesn't exist!" Erik clenched his fists at the sound. Raoul. Which can only mean that he is talking to...*Christine*... Yes, there was her voice, and Erik felt himself relax. She was arguing with the Vicomte about Erik's existence. *So, you haven't forgotten that night after all.* Her next words, however, were like a thousand knives being shoved into his heart. *She remembers my face. And she's disgusted by it.* He would have begun sobbing right then and there, but her mood changed then, as if she were going back into her trance. She began describing his voice and his eyes. *Yes, Christine! You understand...that's who I am! There's hope for us yet!*

His celebration, silent as it was, did not last long. Christine and Raoul began singing to each other. *No, Christine, you're only to sing with me!* Then he realized what they were singing. She wanted to escape from him...from her teacher...and Raoul wanted to protect her. *From what? From me? How dare you think that I would harm her! Never!* Raoul's words were completely undoing everything Erik had sung to her about, and what made matters worse was she was responding to him...smiling, even! Completely helpless, Erik was forced to listen to them, forced to watch their lips touch, forced to sit there silently while his heart shattered inside him. *No, Christine...give me a chance! Give us a chance! Christine...*

Her words were clear enough. She wanted everything that Erik could not give her. Not from behind secret passageways and countless masks. She wanted a life beyond Erik's reach...a life Raoul or anyone else could give her. *But there's music...you're forgetting all about the music...our music!* Just when he thought he couldn't take it anymore, Christine seemed to remember the time. The two quickly left the rooftop, singing as they went.

Slowly, painfully, Erik made his way over to where she had dropped the token of his admiration. The rose was easy to find amid the fallen snow, and he knelt down, fingering it while he took in everything that he had just witnessed. He, like the rose, had just been tossed aside, rejected, all because some newcomer with his flawless face had come in and swept her off her feet. *Don't you understand, Christine? I would have done that for you...I would* have...*if not for this face!* "Christine..." His voice faded, giving way to the flood of tears, and he sobbed openly. No one was there to hear him, and even if they were...he didn't care anymore.

The lovers' voices echoed in his mind. *Stop it! I've been tortured enough!* The spark of anger toward his thoughts was all he needed. *No. This is not over. I will not let her slip through my fingers. Not yet.* He dropped the rose, now without its red petals, and ran across the rooftop. Shouting at the snow-filled sky, he released the pent up anger. As he turned to go back inside, however, he only felt somewhat better. Just then, he heard the unmistakable sound of retreating footsteps through the snow. *Could it be...?* Yes, underneath the bare flower stem was a folded piece of paper. *Who would dare intrude on me?*

"*Dearest Phantom,*

My heart truly aches for what you have just seen. I was only going to thank you for taking care of our little problem, but I must beg of you once more to do another favor. Please, do not do anything you might regret. I said before that Christine is precious to all of us. While my heart breaks for you, please consider her happiness.

Sincerely,

Someone who cares"

Erik felt more exposed than he had ever felt before, even more than he had felt during his time at the fair. Was nothing sacred? Could he not have the privacy he needed? *Who would dare...?* He read the note a second time. *And what of my happiness? For someone who cares, you certainly neglected that! Do I deserve no happiness? Besides, who's to say she won't be happy with me? She won't even give me a chance...* He followed the path of the retreating footprints with his eyes, but by now they were half-buried in snow. No help at all.

He had other things to think about anyway. *I love you, Christine. You'll see. The whole world will see how much I love you.*

Chapter 3: This Is Not Over

Upon his return to the caverns, Erik spent an entire day sobbing and screaming until his throat was sore, and even then, the tears refused to stop. For the first time ever, listening to his music box did not help; the words to the music seemed to taunt him in his mind. Countless times, he cried out for Christine, knowing full well that even if she had been able to hear him, she would not come. Countless other times, he would curse everything about Raoul. *I should be the one protecting her from you! You...coming waltzing into her life with your flowers and money and...passable looks...and expect her to run smiling into your arms! You have not seen her pain! She needs me! We need each other!*

When his voice was spent, he would submerge himself in the deepest part of the lake, letting the coolness wash over him, soothing his aching throat and head, and mixing with the tears still upon his face. He would float there for hours, eyes closed, letting the silence around him inspire his mind to do the same. The last thing he needed would be for his thoughts to start causing him to trip over himself. Only when his body began to shake with cold did he reluctantly emerge from the water. His throat was bad enough without a cold to add onto his problems.

And yet, try as he might, his thoughts would always return to him, and they were filled with a burning question. *Who was it on the rooftop? Who would ever dare to sneak into my presence?* He had kept the last letter. Frustrating as it was, he couldn't get over the signature. "Someone who cares." *But no one cares for me! Christine did...once...but to think she wrote this would be impossible. Antoinette? No, she would have no reason to hide her identity from me...would she?* The questions soon caused him to feel dizzy. He needed to do something about this little distraction, once and for all.

"Dear whomever-you-are,

Whatever game you are playing, it must stop immediately. I have far too much on my mind already to be playing guessing games. I'll thank you to mind your own business from now on.

Sincerely,

O.G."

Erik slipped the note through the vent. He hadn't wanted to leave his caverns for fear of encountering Christine or Raoul, but there was no other way to deliver this one note. He wasted no time in going back into his caverns. He would return tomorrow. Hopefully, this mystery writer would take the hint, and would not reply.

"Dear Phantom,

I must apologize, but I've come too far to stop now. Do not think I am trying to make you guess who I am, if you don't want to. I simply must keep my identity hidden. It would be far too dangerous for me to do otherwise. Please understand.

Sincerely,

A Friend"

"Dear Anonymous,

If it is me you fear, then that is all the more reason for you to name yourself or leave me alone!

Sincerely,

O.G."

"Dear O.G.,

It is not you I fear, dear Phantom. Please, do not ask me again.

Sincerely,

A Friend"

"Dear Phantom,

It has been two months. Where are you?

Sincerely,

Concerned"

Erik sighed as he read the latest note. Yes, it had been two months, hadn't it? He had been too busy writing to notice the passing of time. What had started out as a passing idea the night he had brought Christine downstairs had turned into his biggest plan yet. It was far from being finished, however, which is the only reason why he was wandering the passageways. Again. Sighing, he tossed the note aside.

He would not respond. He needed to focus on his latest project.

"Dear Phantom,

It is now the third month since I last saw you. I am very worried about you. Are you hurt? You must be, if you're allowing Carlotta to snatch back her limelight. Please answer me, Phantom. If I do not hear from you soon, I'm coming down there after you.

Sincerely,

Soneone who cares"

A small debate took place in Erik's mind as he read the note. A small part of him was tempted to remain in hiding, just to see if this mystery writer would in fact go down into his caverns and finally reveal their identity. The majority of himself, however, told him to stick to his plan. His opera was finished. It only needed to be delivered. A new year was upon them, and he knew that the management always threw a party in the opera house. *Do not concern yourself with me any longer, dear writer. You shall see me soon enough.*

Erik's fists clenched at the sound of his song being sung. It had been the first song he'd ever written, and he had delivered a copy to Monsieur Reyer as a gift, to thank him for teaching him how to read and write music. He had not intended for it to be sung at a party of all occasions. This costumed crowd had no idea whatsoever what it was like to hide behind a mask, day after day. Why, even Antoinette had joined in!

He was not here to snatch back his song, however. As he made his way around to the grand staircase, he took in the sight of the extravagant decorations. *So, my managers used my salary on this? They'll not be doing that again, if I have anything to do with it. Which I will.* He clutched the leather folder a little more tightly to him. This was his opera. *His* opera. And there was no way he was going to take the chance of being ignored. Notes could be torn up and tossed aside, and frankly, he was done with them. *You will all see that I am more than an Opera Ghost.*

While he was thinking of notes, a chill ran up his spine. His mystery writer was somewhere in this room. They had to be. He glanced around, studying every face. But it was useless... The masks made it impossible, and he cursed under his breath. Yet another reason why he found a Masquerade a foolish idea, and if the crowd was really paying attention to the words they were singing, they would hear the bitter undertone of it.

But they weren't singing anymore. All of a sudden, all eyes were upon him as he appeared at the top of the staircase. His choice of costume made it impossible for his entrance to be anything but noticeable, for in a room filled with blacks, whites, and golds, his solid Red Death costume definitely stood out. Taking a deep breath, Erik began to descend the stairs. He had an audience, and he wasn't about to disappoint them.

His first words to the crowd were aimed at the managers, his tone a taunting one, laced with inner laughter that they would think he would actually leave them for good. He then threw down the folder in front of them, and he made sure they heard in his voice that this would be their next production and not something they could put off until whenever they felt like using it.

Erik then turned to address the entire crowd, giving them a sarcastic greeting. His eyes then found Carlotta, and a bitter taste entered his mouth. *So many things I have to say to you...where do I begin?* He pointed his sword at her, then to show that he would never harm her, tempting as the thought was, he placed it on her ridiculous hat. Oh, how he wished he could laugh at her face, right then and there! But before he could, Piangi stepped forward. *Ah, you wish to be next, Monsieur? As you wish.* In a few simple lines, Erik managed to name his first casting decision as well as deliver a few insults in response to the singer's futile attempt at stopping him.

Oh, and he couldn't forget about the managers, wasting his salary money on a mere few hours of entertainment. As he told them their place was in an office, he pointed his sword at both of them, and he was pleased when Monsieur Andre's eyes widened in clear understanding.

Lastly, there was Christine. As he turned to face her, the first thing he noticed was how beautiful she looked, as usual. He then noticed that her dear Vicomte was nowhere in sight. All the better, he thought with a smirk, for tonight, not even Christine was above his list of instructions. As he spoke in regards to her, he partially used the same tactic from the mirror. If he showed how upset he was with her or if he made it seem as though she weren't as special to him, she would respond with obedience. Yes, even now, she was walking toward him, staring into his eyes. As he approached her to meet her halfway, it was becoming more and more difficult to feign disinterest. Only when his eyes found the ring on her neck did his anger return. A diamond ring, no doubt a gift from her precious Vicomte. He had heard of such a custom, and he knew that it meant that she belonged to Raoul. *Not quite!* He snatched the ring and chain from her neck, then leaned close to her. "You're mine!" He growled before running back up to the first landing. With a wave of his cape, he dropped through the trap door.

    A second set of footsteps landed beside him, and he quickly moved behind one of the mirrors. *Ah, Vicomte, what a pleasant surprise. Come to play my game, have you?* He inwardly laughed as the Vicomte drew his sword, lunging at the rotating mirrors. Erik had been inspired to build this trap after seeing something similar at the fair, when he was young enough that even the gypsy "master" had thought better than to beat him. It was not often that he had someone trapped in here. He had included two possible outcomes for when he tired of watching them chase their own reflections. One option was for the mirrors to move aside, revealing the way back up to the opera house. He released this outcome for those that encountered this trap by accident. For those that chased him, however, he released a warning. And now, as he tired of watching the insolent Vicomte, he released a warning. A noose fell from the ceiling, just before Antoinette appeared. *About time.* Confident that he was free from the Vicomte for the time being, Erik made his way back to his caverns.

Chapter 4: Twisted Every Way

Just as expected, there was another note waiting for him later that night. For once, he was hoping that there would be. Perhaps the writer would provide a clue as to where they were standing. After reading it, however, he was once again disappointed.

"Dear 'Red Death',

My, what a clever costume you chose! Inspired by Poe, no doubt? So, you wrote an opera in your absence. I cannot wait to see what you've come up with. But please, I beg of you to once again think of Christine's happiness. She is fragile enough as it is.

Sincerely,

A Friend"

Of course I know how fragile she is, which is why she needs me! Erik mentally replied. He could not linger here long, however. He had only come this way because he needed to speak with Antoinette. Although he had no hidden doorway near her quarters, he knew he could get there quickly enough without being seen. Surely, even now, most of the opera house inhabitants would still be in the lobby, talking amongst themselves about what had just transpired. It was a gamble, but thankfully, his prediction came true. Once outside Madame Giry's door, he could hear her voice down the corridor, bidding the younger dancers and chorus girls good night. *Perfect.* Erik slipped through the door and placed himself casually on the sofa.

He did not have to wait long. Not ten minutes later, the door opened once again, followed by a gasp that was soon muffled. "Erik, for goodness sake! Haven't you caused enough excitement for one night?"

"Good evening, Antoinette." Erik greeted her with a smirk, showing her how very unapologetic he was.

"Oh, never mind pleasantries, Erik. It has been a long day, and I would like to get some sleep." The ballet mistress began massaging her forehead.

"You took care of the Vicomte, I trust."

"In what way?" Antonette's eyes grew shifty.

"Has he learned not to tempt death by following me?" Erik's tone of voice grew from friendliness to suspicion.

"I...I very much doubt it, Erik..."

"You're hiding something. Spit it out."

"I...was going to remain silent on your part, Erik. Believe me I tried, but he dragged it out of me!"

"What did you tell him?" Erik was trying to keep his voice calm, but it was becoming very difficult.

"I told him about when I found you...how I brought you here...and how you've lived underneath your whole life..."

"Why? Why did you tell him? So that he can pity me? I tell you, Antoinette, that is the very last thing I need!" He rose from the sofa then, moving dangerously close to Madame Giry.

"Erik, please...my girls are trying to sleep!" Antoinette slipped past him. "I told you. He dragged it out of me. I hoped that it would help him understand you a little better, but..."

"But what?"

"He said that genius has turned to madness. He has decided to stand guard outside Christine's bedchamber from now on."

"Then you had better hope and pray that that is all he is planning." With that, Erik left the ballet mistress to ponder his latest threat. He had hoped to question her about the mysterious notes, but once again, thoughts of Christine took priority.

He returned to his caverns only to change into warmer clothes. He planned on spending the rest of the night in the stables, where the cool January air was sure to sooth his thoughts better than the damp air of the caves. Normally, he would have gone to the rooftop, but after the last intrusion, he was not about to face that memory again.

Like most other nights, he did not know as to whether or not he slept. Try as he might to avoid nightmare-filled sleep, exhaustion in his body sometimes became too overwhelming to fight it. All he remembered was closing his eyes but refusing to think. The mystery surrounding the notes was beginning to add headaches every time he thought about it.

Shortly before dawn, the sound of footsteps forced him to alertness. Peering out of the shadows, he almost let out a moan. *Christine.* Intrigue quickly turned into concern, however, as he became more aware of the surroundings. *She's alone. Hardly dressed for this cold weather...where on earth is she off to...alone?* For a moment, anger flashed inside him. *Where's your precious Vicomte now? If he really cares about you, would he not be at your side this very moment?* As Christine approached the carriage driver without hesitation, Erik had to practically bite his tongue to keep from crying out. *Have you lost your mind, girl? What's come over you, that you don't have a thought for your safety?* The driver accepted her meager fare, and she told him she wished to go to the cemetery. *To visit your father, no doubt. You should not go alone, dear girl.* As she disappeared to fetch a cloak, Erik saw his chance. Grabbing a shovel, he slowly crept toward the driver, now distracted with getting the horses and carriage ready. Slowly, he raised up the shovel...

"Don't do it!" A voice whispered. Chills ran up his spine as he whirled around to face the source. Numerous shadowy stalls were all that met his gaze, however. Turning back, he saw that the opportunity was lost, and he quickly ran back into hiding. *Who would DARE...* Helplessly, Erik watched as Christine got into the carriage and was soon gone. *Whoever you are, you WILL pay!* Before he could begin his search, Raoul darted out of seemingly nowhere.

"Christine!" he urgently called. The carriage was far from sight, however, and he leaped onto the nearest horse(it would be a white one, Erik noted bitterly) and galloped after her. Finally alone, Erik used every bit of self-training and instinct to search the stables. Time and time again, he thought he heard footsteps running through the hay, but his search turned out to be fruitless. At this point, he was seeing nothing but red before his eyes. He needed to scream. He needed to punch something. But to do so would draw attention to himself and betray his hiding spot. And so he made his way back down to the caverns in record time. Neglecting his boat, he dove into the lake fully clothed. But even after hours of swimming, he was still as frustrated as ever. Not only had this mystery writer taken away his sense of privacy, they had robbed him of the one opportunity to be Christine's shoulder as she grieved. *Now, let it be war upon you...whoever you are!*

"Writer,

You try my patience. It is time you learned to fear me. You will end this game of yours. Do not forget what I am capable of.

Sincerely,

O.G."

This time, Erik did not return to his caverns after delivering his note. He did not care if it took days or months, he would see who was behind the letters and distractions, once and for all. He was used to going hungry. Many times, his music would consume so much of him that his stomach didn't even growl once. And so he resolved to sit behind the vent, not shifting his gaze once. To be sure, his thoughts kept returning to Christine, but each time he was tempted to look for her, he would realize that had he not been so focused on Christine, he would have figured out this mystery right from the beginning. He refused to think of the soprano as a distraction, however. She was so much more than that to him, and nothing would ever change that.

Five hours into his watch, he heard footsteps and muffled voices enter the room on the other side of the vent. *Finally!* Leaning forward, he peered through the vent. His eager smirk soon melted away, however. It's only Little Giry...and *Christine!* Half-tempted to crash through the wall, he forced himself to sit and listen. "Oh, Christine, must you? It's so soon!" the young dancer was sobbing.

"I'm afraid so, Meg. I just can't stay here any longer...not in the opera house...not even in Paris...I just can't!" Tears were also streaming down Christine's face. *Oh, Vicomte, if you are the cause for her tears...you had better sleep with both eyes open!*

"Why, Christine? You must tell me! You could always tell me everything before."

"Meg, do you remember what I told you? About my Angel of Music?" Erik could not help noticing the subtle roll of Marguerite's eyes.

"Yes, I remember."

"Well, this morning, I went to visit my father's grave. I...I said good bye for good...and I told him..." Christine now shook with her sobs, and her friend gently lowered her to a sofa. "I told him to take back the Angel...that I don't need him anymore..." Hearing this, Erik now had to bite down hard on his tongue. *Of course you need me, Christine! You've always needed me! And I need you, don't you see that?*

"Christine, Angel or not, we both saw the man dressed as Red Death. Everyone saw him."

"Which is why I need to leave, Meg. I must. Raoul followed me to the cemetery. When the worst of my crying was over, he said we could be married and leave Paris right away. He can take me away from all that I fear."

"As well as all that you love." Marguerite lowered her head then, and Erik could not tell if she had meant to say that out loud.

"Oh, Meg, I wish there was some other way...it's not that I don't care about you...this is just something I need to do. Please tell me you understand?"

"What about 'Don Juan Triumphant'? Won't you at least sing one more time?"

"Oh, Meg...I really don't know. He wrote it...I can only imagine what he might do..."

"To you? Oh, Christine, I think everyone saw the look on his face when he saw you. I am sure he would not harm you. Please. Talk it over with Raoul. Just don't go. Not yet."

"I'll think about it, Meg." Drying their tears, the two friends embraced. Erik couldn't take it anymore. The writer's mystery would have to wait, once again. A song had just formed itself in his mind, and he wasn't about to sing it where Christine might hear.

Once again, he made his way down to the caverns, and this time, he took the boat. Once in his living quarters, he crouched at the lakeside, moving his fingers through the water while his heart and his mind finished writing the song. Finally confident, he began singing a song, telling of how he'd been so alone for so long, listening to the music only he could hear. He sang of how he'd first encountered her...How they shared so much pain and loneliness... How he longed to share with the world...

By the last chorus, he had made his way over to his cluttered desk, and as the last note was sung, he dropped his face into his hands. Oh, he had something planned, all right. He had hoped it wouldn't come to this, but Christine's revelation of her plans put a new urgency to his. Have no fear, Little Giry. Christine won't be going anywhere.

Chapter 5: I'm Not Ready

"Dear Phantom,

Please know that I did not mean to anger you. However, since I did anyway, I am truly sorry. I only meant to keep anyone from getting hurt. If it helps, there has been talk about a plot against you that will take place opening night. I felt I should warn you. Please be careful.

Sincerely,

A Friend"

  Erik crumpled up the note. Did this writer think so little of him that they thought he didn't know everything that went on within the opera house? *And even if that is not the case, 'sorry' does not return that opportunity to me! 'Sorry' does not erase the tears on Christine's face! Had I gone with her, we could have comforted each other! But now it's too late, all because of you!* He could not ignore the fact that Raoul had followed Christine, but he could have dealt with the insolent youth easily when the time came.

He did not have time to dwell on what might have been, however. Erik knew that the police had been sent for, in full force, to surround the opera house from the inside out. He would not disappoint the extra audience members, however. There were two options, and the choice was completely in Christine's hands. Should she go along with him, they would deliver the finest performance yet. But should anything go wrong...should she force him to it, he would give all of Paris something that they would never forget.

But he had to move quickly if it was going to work. There were only two measly hours before curtain went up, and he had seen Christine go into the chapel. He would have gone in with her, or at least into the passageway behind its walls, but he had to take care of something else first.

Once everything was in place, he debated leaving a note for the mysterious writer. He decided against it, however. Whoever it was must surely be preparing for the opera and would have no time to sneak around. *Good.* Everything depended on a smooth flow of events, and if the writer valued their life and those of everyone inside the opera house, they would not be interfering.

He could not go without leaving one last note with Antoinette, however. She had been too much of a help to him to not deserve a final goodbye. In the short note, he left all his banked salary money to her, for whatever needs might arise after tonight.

As he was moving through the passageways, he caught a glimpse of Raoul through one of his many peepholes. The Vicomte was just entering the chapel, and once again, Erik was left debating as to whether or not he should listen in. But no, he had one more trip down to the caverns to make. *Oh, let them say their good byes. What's the harm in that?* Hoping upon hope that his thoughts were right in their assumption, he made his way back to his living quarters. These would be his last few moments alone down here, for when he returned, Christine would be with him. Whichever way she chose, she would be safe with him forever, and the writer's letters would stop (whether by unfortunate mishap or final realization on their part).

In these last few moments alone in his caverns, Erik adjusted his wig and switched into a black 'Don Juan' mask, while in the back of his mind, he couldn't stop thinking about Christine. *Finally, Christine, we'll be together, alone to sing our music forever. You'll be free of all the pressures of living in the public's eye. It will just be the two of us, and all you need to do is sing for me. In time, you'll learn to love me. I just know it.*

From his perch in the shadows backstage, Erik cringed as Carlotta sang with the chorus. At least she didn't grab the role of Aminta. Yes, for once, everything was going according to plan. Everything was going smoothly. *Too smoothly.* There was no time to back out now, however. The curtain beside him parted, and Piangi appeared, laughing. With no hesitation, Erik jumped down on top of him. Even if the writer tried to interfere now, there was no time to do anything about it. Tugging once more on the rope, Erik stood up, listening as Christine's sweet soprano voice penetrated his thoughts. *This is it. No turning back. You're on.* He could not think about the full house of opera goers. He could not take into consideration the length of time that had passed since he was in front of a crowd of this size, let alone the circumstances surrounding that last time. No, this was his opera and his cue. Taking a deep breath, he stepped through the curtain.

As scripted, he quickly dismissed 'Passarino', leaving himself alone with Christine. As he sang his part, he watched her finger the rose in her hand. He wondered if she recognized it, but she seemed extra nervous as he came closer. *No matter. She's here. She wants to sing.* As she turned to face him, a trace of recognition flashed across her face. He brought his index finger to his mouth. *Don't scream. We're just going to sing a song. That is all.*

Seeming to understand his unspoken message, Christine climbed back into her role and flew into her part perfectly. Pleased with her obedience, Erik stole a glance at Box Five. *My Box Five.* The Vicomte was there, as usual, and Erik inwardly smirked at his widened eyes. *You see, Vicomte? She does care about me. Had she not, she would not have come.* His attention was quickly drawn back to Christine, for she had climbed so far into her character that Erik felt himself begin to sweat. *This is what you wanted, isn't it?* But no matter how many times he'd imagined this, it did not compare to what he was seeing right before his very eyes. *The bridge, Erik. Climb up to the bridge. And for goodness sake, breathe! This is just an opera...your opera...do not mess it up!*

As soon as the two met in the middle of the bridge, Erik grabbed Christine from behind and pressed her to him. At that moment, everything else seemed to melt away. Whatever he had planned for the rest of the opera was quickly forgotten. It was just the two of them now. No going back now. Slowly, softly, he began singing into her ear the song that had caused her to give her heart to Raoul. *If it worked for him, surely it will work for me. After all, she loves my voice. How can she deny me now?* As he sang to her, caressing her neck and hair, her eyes fluttered open, as if waking up from a dream. Slowly, she turned to face him. *She's choosing me! Say yes, Christine! Say you'll love me!* Yes, even now, she lifted her hand up to his face.

And then there was a draft, a cold, familiar draft on the right side of his face, followed by echoes upon echoes of screams. It was as if his past was coming back to haunt him, mixing in with the screams of the present. *How could you, Christine? In my caverns was one thing. But here? Now? Did you not learn? Did you not see my pain before?* A look of apology came over her face, but it was too late. The betrayal had taken place, and now, he could see the police rushing toward them. *Not so fast.* Gripping Christine tightly to him, he released the chandelier and the trap door beneath them. As they dropped, the added layer of screams coming from the house served to prove his distraction was a success.

Once they landed, Erik wasted no time in making his way back to his caverns, gripping Christine tightly by her wrist. There was no time for pleasantries, unlike last time. Unlike before, this was not the time for soothing songs and comfort. *Darkness is the reality of my life. The sooner you understand that, the better.* "Please...Angel...my feet...you're hurting me..." Christine interrupted his train of thought. Quickly, Erik glanced down and inwardly kicked himself. *Of course. She's in bare feet. The way I wrote it. Curses!* Thankfully, they were at the lake by now, and he paused only to pick her up and place her into the boat. As he brought them across, he couldn't help noticing her clutching her wrist.

"I did not mean to hurt you, Christine." It was the closest he could bring himself to apologizing. She remained silent, save for her breathless sobs. *Is this how you really wanted it, Erik?* Once again cursing his thoughts, he reminded them that it was Christine who chose this...it was Christine who had exposed his face to the world, yanking from him every ounce of security. *If only you had let me wait until you were ready to see...if only you had understood from the start...and you still don't understand, do you? No. Ripping off my mask just now proved it.* He would make her understand. She was here with him now, and she would listen.

Finally reaching the stony bank, he pulled her up and out of the boat. Only when they had come to the wax figure and the wedding dress did he stop and turn her to face him. "Why did you do that, Christine? Why? I have built a home down here because there's no other place for me. Darkness holds the only compassion I've found. I thought you were different. I thought you would understand!" His words were met with silence; Christine was still trying to catch her breath from the journey. With a sigh, Erik lowered his gaze. "Go...put that dress on. I'll turn away." Leaving her side, he retrieved the diamond ring from the top of his desk. Pleased to hear her movements to obey him, he sat down and stared at the ring. *You know, Erik, you're not really showing that you love her. Must you treat her so rough?*

Sighing, he realized he had to agree with his thoughts this time. He was treating her rough, and he hated it. Christine was not like all the others. She deserved much more. *Yet, she betrayed me. How else will she learn not to cross me?* But was this really the way to begin their future?

His torturous thoughts were interrupted by the sound of her descending the stairs. *She's as beautiful as I pictured it.* He could not linger on her beauty, however. He hadn't pictured forcing her to wear the dress. He hadn't pictured dragging her down here against her will. Most of all, he hadn't pictured her next words. "So, I'm to be your next victim? Is that it?" *Must you put it that way?*

"You would not feel like a victim if it wasn't for this face. If not for this face, you would love me." He reached out to touch her, but she turned her face away. With a sigh, Erik turned to take the veil off the wax figure. "Even my mother hated me for my face. I do not expect you to love me right away. You have an eternity to get used to the sight of it." As he placed the veil on her head, he turned her to face him. Her eyes widened, but not from fear. As he looked into her eyes, he saw the truth. *Pity.* He chose to ignore it. *If I expect her to overlook my face, surely I can overlook her pity.* He moved his hand down to grasp hers, and into it, he placed the ring. *You're mine.*

She moved past him then, sliding the veil off her head and letting it drop to the floor. Pulling a curtain off of one of his many mirrors, she told him that it wasn't the face that was the problem. "It's within your soul that your true scars are." *No...that can't be the problem. You had to have seen into my soul every time I sang to you...you loved me then!* Before he could ponder her words any further, the sound of splashing footsteps drew his attention to the iron gate. The Vicomte, soaked completely from head to toe, stumbled through the lake, finally leaning on the gate to catch his breath. Erik's mood changed completely then. *So, you've come to play my games yet again, Vicomte? I would have thought you'd have tired of them after the last time.*

"What a pleasant surprise! Come to witness the wedding, have you?" Erik wrapped his arm around Christine. At this, the Vicomte seemed to gain back his strength.

"Do what you like to me, just let her go!"

"Raoul, it's useless!" Christine called out, and Erik smirked. *Better listen to her, Vicomte. She speaks the truth!*

"Don't you understand? I love her! Have you any compassion?" *Wrong choice of words, dear Vicomte!*

"The world didn't have any compassion for me!" Erik roared. As Raoul continued his plea, a new idea struck Erik's mind. Stepping away from Christine, he pulled the lever to open the gate. Seeming to have no thoughts to his own safety, the Vicomte stepped through. *That's it, just a little bit closer...* As the gate closed, Erik bent down to retrieve the rope he kept hidden beneath the shallow water for such a time as this. "Why would I harm Christine when it is you who has come between us?" As he spoke, he threw the rope around the stunned youth. He heard Christine gasp behind him. *Oh, I won't hurt him, Christine. Not yet at least.* To be sure, he could have snuffed out Raoul's life right then and there, and a good part of him wanted to do just that. But he was done forcing Christine to love him. This way, she would prove to him that his love was returned. Binding the Vicomte to the iron gate, he gave her the choice. "You want his freedom? Love me then! Refuse me and he dies! This is the choice you have to make!" He watched as tears began streaming down Christine's face.

"I hate you." *I would think much longer before making such a statement. Perhaps a visual will help.* He moved behind her to where he had another lasso stored. As she continued to express her hatred, Erik made his way back toward his prisoner. Slipping the rope around the Vicomte's neck, he tightened it just enough to show that he wasn't joking.

"Why make her lie just to save me?" *For someone in your position, you'd be wise to choose your last words carefully.* To enforce his point, he gave the rope another tug while making his way back toward Christine.

"You tricked me into blindly giving you my mind." Christine glared at him through tear-filled eyes.

"I'm growing impatient. You'd better decide." He pulled on the rope on more time, not taking his eyes off of her. She hesitated only a moment before her face changed. As she approached him, the look on her face matched what he had seen on the rooftop that painful night. Her words, however, were filled with pity. Not love. Not compassion. Pity. But he couldn't speak. He couldn't breathe. She slipped the ring onto her finger before reaching her hands up to his face. Without a mask, he knew there were no other motives here. *She wants to touch me. She's choosing me.* At that moment, she lifted her face and touched her lips to his. *A kiss! She's kissing me!* His face must have reflected his disbelief then, for she kissed him a second time. It seemed forced, however, and as she pulled away, she gave him a careful half-smile as her eyes held a question in them.

"Was that enough?" They seemed to ask. *Was it?* No. If he set Raoul free now but kept Christine with himself, their pain would be hanging over his

head for the rest of his life. *They belong together.* That painful realization hit him then, and there was no ignoring the truth. *You need to let them go. It's time to say good bye.* He didn't want to. He didn't want to be parted from her forever. He was far from ready to say good bye. Yet, even now, words from the mysterious letters came back to him. "*She is precious to all of us...she's fragile...don't forget her happiness...*" As much as he wanted her with him, he could never harm her. Not physically, and certainly not emotionally. *She deserves so much more than you can give her.* Yes, he needed to do this. He needed to let her be with the one she truly loved.

And so he would say good bye. Tears streaming down his face, he dropped the rope and began walking away. Unable to control his sobs, he ordered them to take the boat and leave him. *Go now, before I change my mind!* Music. He needed music. Half-dizzy from his breaking heart and from the feeling of her lips still tingling on his, he wound up the music box, collapsing to the closest chair. The music washed over him then, as it had so many times before, and he became lost inside it. All too soon, it slowed to a stop, and he glimpsed a small movement out of the corner of his eyes. *Christine. She hasn't left.* Even now, after his realization, his heart scrambled to grab onto any shred of hope left. *Just one thread...that's all I need...* As Christine approached him, she lifted her hands to show that she was removing the ring. Slowly, she reached down and lifted his hand. As he had done only minutes before, she closed his hand around the ring. No words were spoken. None were needed. She pulled away, returning to the boat and her future. Her message was clear enough. *It's over.*

Erik stood and walked over to the edge of the platform. As painful as it was to see the two of them together, he wasn't ready to let her out of his sight. They were singing again, and the words were all too familiar. Just before they disappeared around the corner, Christine, the love of his life and the muse to his songs, took one last look over her shoulder. *Farewell, my teacher, my Angel of Music,* her eyes seemed to say. *No...not yet...don't go...* But it was too late. The boat was gone, and with it went his heart, shattered into millions of pieces.

Overcome with rage and heartbreak, Erik lost complete control of his actions. It was as if his very soul had gone with Christine, and all that remained was his broken shell of a body, smashing into mirror after mirror. *What's the point? All of this...every inch...was for you, Christine! It was all for you!*

Only when he felt a hand on his shoulder did he snap back into reality.

Chapter 6: I Know Who You Are

Erik shoved the hand away. *You won't get me that easily!* He finished smashing the mirror that would open up his escape route. As millions of shards of glass fell to the floor around him, he inwardly said farewell to everything that was familiar. Secure. Safe. *Christine.* Now that she was gone, he no longer felt that he could call this place home. Without her, it was once again nothing but a cold, dark prison. And so he took a single step into the unknown darkness before him.

Before he could move any further, he again felt a hand tugging on his arm. "Please Monsieur. Don't go." Erik spun around at the familiar voice.

"Marguerite, this is no place for a little girl like you. Where I go is no concern of yours."

"Oh, but it is, Monsieur. It has been my concern for the past three years."

"What are you talking abou-" *Three years. The notes. Little Marguerite Giry was behind them? No. It can't be.*

"Oh...your hands...what have you done to them?" Her voice pulled him out of his thoughts, and he glanced down. In his rage, he had been smashing his mirrors with his bare hands, and now they were covered in blood. Before he could speak, he heard the sound of the approaching mob. *There's no way I'm leaving here without some answers.* Gripping the little dancer's shoulder, he ignored the pain in his hands and pulled her through the doorway. As soon as the curtain was closed, he pushed her against the stone wall.

"So. You're the writer? You're the one who has done nothing but interfere in my personal business?"

"Yes, Monsieur." She met his gaze evenly, which made him all the more angry at her.

"Give me one good reason why I shouldn't kill you now." His voice was a low growl, and despite the pain surging through his hands, he gripped her throat tight enough so that she would know he was dead serious.

"Your hands for one. For another, you'd never do it."

"Do you have any idea as to what you've done? You had no right...no right poking your nose into my business!"

"I had every right! Christine is my best friend...almost my sister! I was only trying to help...I didn't want anyone getting hurt..."

"Except someone did end up getting hurt, didn't they?"

"That would not have happened if you had read my last note."

"Of course I read it. I simply chose to ignore it. Besides, I was fully aware of the plan, and as you saw, I was ready for it."

"No...there was one after that one...it was last-minute, and I tried to get it to you before..." His eyes already adjusted to the darkness, Erik watched the dancer reach into her belt and withdraw a white square of paper. "It's too dark to read it here...what I was trying to say is that I overheard Christine and Raoul. They were planning to humiliate you...to give the police time to capture you."

"And had you not been playing games and hiding your identity, you could have very well come and found me instead of shoving that piece of information through a vent!"

"I'm sorry...I..."

"Come with me. We'll continue this discussion further in." Not giving her a chance to reply, he forced her hand behind her back and shoved her forward. After several dizzying twists and turns, the passageway ended at a wall*(or so it would seem to anyone foolish enough to venture into this darkness)*. Pressing a single stone, the wall opened up to reveal a room large enough to house him comfortably for any length of time necessary. What he hadn't planned on was having a prisoner. *Well it's her own fault.* Throwing her to the floor, he crossed the room to the opposite wall, trying to comprehend all that had just taken place.

"Please...do you have a candle? Some light?"

"Why? So you can see my face?"

"Yes." The single word caught him off-guard. He turned to face her, thankful that she could not see his confusion.

"Why? So you can laugh at it?"

"Of course not. Please, I...I'd just like to see..." An exasperated sigh escaped his throat at the innocence in her voice. After lighting a single candle, he brought it over to where he had built a small fireplace. Setting fire to the pile of scrap wood, he set the candle on the table. He watched her face as her eyes adjusted to the light. There was no fear or disgust. Instead, it appeared as though she was studying him as much as he was studying her.

"I'll not have you staring at my face, either." He turned his face away.

"Of course not. You're a human being, not something to be put on display."

"I suppose your mother told you about my past, then?"

"Not directly..." Erik noticed her shift her gaze to the stone floor.

"So, I'm not the only one you snoop on." As a thick silence fell upon them, the stinging in his hands returned to the front of his mind, and he attempted to hide the wince on his face. Silently, Marguerite got to her feet and walked over to where an underground spring fed into a pool of water. Ripping off a small corner of the bottom of her blouse, she dipped it in the water and approached Erik. Puzzled, Erik was forced to do nothing but watch her. Only when the damp cloth touched his hand did he roar in pain. "What on earth are you doing?"

"Your hands, Monsieur. They must be cleaned. If there are any other scraps of cloth here, I could bandage them up for you." Erik yanked the cloth out of her hands while shoving her away.

"I'll thank you to not touch me again. Do not forget that you are my prisoner, and until I figure out how I'm going to deal with you, you are to remain silent. Am I understood, Little Giry?"

"Yes, Monsieur. Forgive me." Lowering her head, the dancer returned to her initial spot on the floor beside the secret door. Erik turned his back to her, concealing his action of dabbing at the wounds on his hands. Once he was sure he had gotten all the glass out, he opened one of the chests he had stored and retrieved an extra shirt. Ripping it to shreds, he selected two strips and wrapped them around his hands.

"There, you see? My hands are fine." He flashed a smirk at the dancer. She did not respond. She didn't even look up. In the tense silence, Erik was forced to once again replay the evening's events in his mind. Within moments, the silence was broken as the sound of carefree sobs echoed off the walls of the small room. Turning to scold Marguerite, he saw that she was curled up on the floor, and he realized that the sobs were his own.

Splashing. He was drowning, but his face was dry and warm. Dark, and yet there was a faint light coming from somewhere. Music. Where have you gone, my music? My muse...my love...Christine. Erik's eyes fluttered open. *Fool! Why did you let yourself sleep? You know what happens when you do!* As he sat up, his neck felt stiff from the stone floor. The sound of splashing water continued, and he slowly turned to face the pool. "Just what do you think you are doing, Little Giry?" The dancer jumped at his voice. She was kneeling at the pool side, face and hands dripping with the cool water. There was a red tint to her face that he hadn't noticed before. *Blood.* Yes, he had touched her with his wounded hands, but nowhere above her throat. The smashing mirrors. She had gotten too close, in more ways than one.

"I didn't mean to wake you, Monsieur. Please...ignore me. You need your rest."

"Do not tell me what I may or may not need. You may know plenty more than you should, but do not pretend to know how I feel." Erik stood, stretching his body to prevent any further stiffness.

"I...would have prepared something for breakfast, but I do not know where you keep your food." *Good. One more thing you do not know about me.*

"I am not in the least bit hungry."

"I know I'm supposed to be your prisoner, and I know there are many things you are capable of, Monsieur. Cruelty cannot be one of them."

"Do you really want to be testing that, Little Giry?" Silence followed his question. *Good choice.* "If you must know, I have enough food provisions stored for two meals a week. However, as we will both be in need of nourishment, you will only be eating once a week. Take it or go hungry. I do not care either way."

"If I'm really so much of a burden to you, Monsieur, then you would not have brought me here."

"I will get to my reasons when I get to them. All you need to know is that when this is over, you will regret ever touching your pen to a single scrap of paper."

"And all you need to know is that you don't need to put up a brave front for me. I saw what happened last night, and I can only imagine how much you are hurting. Do not keep your tears bottled up inside you, or you'll eventually do something you'll regret."

"Did I not order you to not tell me what to do?" Erik roared, but the mere mention of the previous night's events caused something to burst inside him. All of a sudden, he couldn't breathe. Something was crushing his chest. *My heart cannot be broken any further!* Pent up sobs were begging for escape, and a lump was growing in his throat. He couldn't let the dancer see his weakness, however. "Turn your face away!" He managed. Marguerite only blinked at him. "I'll not say it again! Turn away!" Slowly, she did as she was ordered, and Erik collapsed onto the floor, burying his head in his hands. *Curse you, Marguerite! Curse you for being right!*

Chapter 7: I Want Answers

Erik awoke with a start, then closed his eyes again with a groan. Had he really allowed sleep to overtake him again? *And what on earth caused me to wake up?* Just then, he felt a soft tingling on the right side of his face. Slowly, he opened his eyes, and everything returned to him in that moment. *Christine's gone. I am in hiding once again. And Little Giry is caressing my face. What..?* Reaching up, he grasped her wrist. "You're awake..." Her voice was weak, but full of relief.

"And you, Mademoiselle, are touching me, after I specifically told you not to." His body felt weak, but he was not about to admit it.

"Monsieur, you've been asleep for several days. You would not stop crying...you even became feverish. I thought..." Fresh tears shone on her face, and it was at that moment when Erik saw how pale and thin she had become.

"If you're trying to starve yourself to make me feel sorry for you..."

"You never told me where the food was, Monsieur." *Didn't I?* His head was spinning, but he fought it.

"Lift the four center stones under the table. They are not as heavy as they look." He would not have given her that information so quickly, but he needed her to be distracted by something. While her back was turned, Erik rolled over and closed his eyes. *Christine, where are you? Now is when I need you the most...* All of a sudden, he realized he hadn't been resting on the cold stone floor. Every single spare blanket he had stored was spread out around him; the thickest one under him, one rolled up for a pillow, and the thinnest one covering his legs. A new realization hit him then, and he paled. "Marguerite, where is my shirt?"

"Hanging to dry on the mantle. I washed it, since it was soaked through with sweat and tears."

"That had better be all you removed."

"The only other things were your boots. As I said, you were feverish." Marguerite approached him then with a bowl of water and a tiny piece of bread.

"I told you before, I am not hungry."

"Monsieur, that was days ago! You must eat."

"Why? What do I have to live for anymore?"

"Please, Monsieur?" Her wide brown eyes were even more enhanced against the paleness of her face, and he immediately saw Antoinette in them. Sighing, he sat up and took the food and water from her. It was then that he noticed his hands, now free of the bandages, but still bearing the scars. "If your hands are still in pain, I can find more cloth for bandages. I had to toss the other ones into the fire...they were too soaked with blood."

"Are you going to just sit there talking, or are you going to eat?" Oh, he was in pain, all right, but not in his hands. An all-too-familiar headache was returning. In the silence, he could only imagine all that had taken place while he was asleep. He pictured her maneuvering the blanket underneath him, almost laughing at the comical picture that came to his mind. He thought of her tugging off his boots and his soaked shirt, and he wondered if when he was dreaming of being thrown out into the rain, she was actually rubbing cool water on his feverish body. At that thought, he did not know if he was blushing or growing paler. *I would not mind so much, if you were only Christine.* With thoughts of his love fresh in his mind, he finished his meal quickly before laying back down, his back to the dancer. *Oh, Christine...if only...* A song came to his mind then, its words telling of longing to see her one more time...To hear her voice again...But knowing it could never be...

"That's lovely, Monsieur." Marguerite's voice interrupted his train of thought. *Was I just singing?*

"You will forget you ever heard that, Little Giry."

"You mustn't be ashamed, Monsieur. It is just the two of us...and besides. I told you before that I love your voice."

"What you heard was meant for Christine and Christine only. Not some eavesdropping nuisance of a dancer!"

"But you sang for hundreds of people the other night..." *My, but she's gained back her strength quickly.*

"That was for Christine as well! Don't you understand? I gave her my music...We spent all those nights singing together...she was supposed to love me in return. Instead, she betrayed me!" Through the new flood of tears, Erik watched as Marguerite got up and retrieved a cloth from the mantle. Gingerly, she handed it to him.

"For your tears..." Erik yanked it from her.

"Why couldn't you leave me alone?"

"I did nothing but care! Why are you so angry with me?"

"Oh, where do I begin?" Erik scoffed. "When she told you about me, you tried to turn her against me!"

"I did not! If anything, I was amazed by how you shaped her voice into what it is. I was never against you, Monsieur."

"Then why would you tell her she was dreaming, if you knew very well that I'm real?"

"That's just it, Monsieur. I knew you were real, not the spirit of her father."

"Do you really think she would have opened up to me if she knew it was a lonely, disfigured man singing to her? You were always meddling and not thinking that I might have a reason for every single thing I did!"

"What was I supposed to do, Monsieur? Just sit back and let you deceive Christine and take her away from everything she loves?"

"She would have learned to love me, if she had just given me a chance!"

"Why would you ask her to do that when she loved Raoul even before she came here?"

"Is it so wrong of me to want to be loved?" The question was out before Erik could stop it, and he cringed at how weak it made him sound.

"No, Monsieur. It's not wrong to want it. But it is wrong when you try to force someone to love you. True love is not selfish, and it is not built on lies." By now, Erik was sobbing so much that he couldn't speak. He wanted to slap her for being so bold, but he barely had the strength to bring the cloth up to his stinging eyes. *You're wrong, Little Giry! You know nothing of love!*

For the rest of the day, the two sat in silence, as if an invisible wall stood between them. Erik did not dare to speak; he did not trust his raw emotions. His only pleasure came from the fact that, for once, Marguerite seemed smart enough to keep silent. He did not have the patience to deal with her. Every ounce of energy was used to force himself to stay awake. He had never been able to fully embrace sleep anyway, let alone with a blond-haired dancer watching his every move.

And that was another thing. Had he not instructed that she not stare at him? But what could he say? This was Antoinette's daughter, and he could already tell that she had inherited her mother's stubbornness. Besides, he had given her nothing else to do but stare at him. *You brought her here for a reason, Erik. Ask her some of your questions!* Erik cleared his throat, causing Marguerite to jump an inch. "Suppose you tell me how you came to write those letters?" Marguerite took a deep breath before speaking.

"I've been curious about you my whole life. For as long as I can remember, whispered stories of you were always on everyone's lips. Only when you pulled one of your pranks did you become real to me...to all of us. I was frightened at first, but over time, I began looking forward to the breaks in the monotony. Then I began seeing a change in Christine. She began singing again...and she was no longer as sad. I started following her into the chapel whenever I could, and I...I could hear you, Monsieur. You'd be singing together such beautiful music..."

"Skip to the first note, Mademoiselle." Erik growled. *I do not need to be reminded of what I once had!*

"Right. That was shortly after Carlotta arrived, wasn't it? Yes, after the second rehearsal. She had come out on stage, screaming about some dresses all torn to shreds. I knew it couldn't have been anyone else but you... I knew I couldn't be the only one who found her voice awful. I had to let you know you were appreciated."

"Just the one note would have been sufficient, Little Giry."

"After the first note, I don't know... I guess I discovered how much I enjoyed writing it and the thrill of delivering it. I suppose it was another way of expressing myself...reaching out to someone who would listen." Erik looked up at her then. Had that not been exactly what he had been trying to do? But no...he would not give her the satisfaction of knowing that they shared anything. Still, he was intrigued, and he realized that more questions were coming to his mind as she answered them.

"And suppose I had never gotten those letters, Marguerite? Suppose your effort had turned out to be nothing but a waste?"

"That made no difference, at least not at first. Those first letters were simply a way for me to get things off my chest."

"What changed?" There was that weakness again. It was as if her curiosity was a disease, contagious and spreading to him.

"That night Christine disappeared...I found your passageway behind the mirror. I got as far as the lake, and I could hear your voice echoing off the walls. I knew you were singing to her...your voice was so soothing that I could not picture her doing anything but melting from the sound of it. And then I thought that maybe my notes to you could be more than just a way of expressing myself."

"You meant to protect her from me, is that it? You're no different than the Vicomte if that is the case!"

"Monsieur, I didn't know what would happen. I know Christine better than I know you, and so I was only thinking of her." At this, Erik sighed. *She has a point there.* There was so much more he wanted to ask, but his headache had only grown worse. Not wanting Marguerite to see his weakness, he forced all thoughts of pain to the back of his mind.

"Fetch my shirt, Little Giry, and you had better think twice of ever touching it again." His sudden change of subject was met with slight hesitation, but she shook off her confusion quickly and moved to obey. As she handed over the garment, he locked his eyes on hers, making sure that she saw the dead seriousness in them. "This discussion is far from over, Marguerite." With that, he turned his back to her, dismissing her silently. He heard her settling in for the night across the room, and only when she was silent did he slip the clean shirt over his torso. *Sleep easy, Little Giry, for that will serve as your only escape from me!*

Chapter 8: Whose Fault is it Really?

Erik watched her toss and turn throughout the night. Occasionally, she would let out a tiny whimper, and in the firelight, he could see a few stray tears falling down her face. Whatever she was dreaming about, he wouldn't allow himself to care. *It's her own fault.* Instead, he turned his attention to the fire, feeding it a few more scraps of wood. As he watched the flames consume the fresh wood, he wondered about the damages upstairs. *Did Christine make it out safely?* Perhaps she did and that foolish Vicomte did not? A smirk appeared on his face then, but it quickly disappeared. *Even if that's true, she would still hold you responsible.* Sighing, he got to his feet and began pacing the floor. His legs were stiff and his stomach growled, but he ignored it. At least he had an endless supply of water. Yes, a cool drink would soothe his aching head.

Stepping carefully so as not to wake the sleeping dancer, he made his way over to the pool and drenched his head in the water before taking long, deep sips. Finally satisfied, he suddenly became aware that he was not the only one awake. He turned to face Marguerite, ready to scold her for staring at him. Instead of watching him, however, she had her back to him, arms on her knees, and her chin resting on top of them. The few stray tears had become a steady flow, but her sobbing was silent. *I don't care. I don't care, I do not care!* "What could you possibly have to cry about, Marguerite? You being here was your own doing."

"Forgive me, Monsieur...it's silly really..."

"No one cries over anything silly, Little Giry."

"It was just a dream...several actually, and they were all about my mother. First I saw her being burnt alive, and I heard her ashes crying out my name...and then I saw her sitting alone in an empty room...crying for me..."

"As I said. This is your own doing." Erik stood back up and walked across the room from her.

"The fire wasn't my doing, Monsieur." At this, Erik whirled around, glaring daggers in her direction.

"It would not be wise for you to test me, Little Giry. I may have started that fire, true enough, but had you made the effort to seek me out with your most recent bit of information, I would never have taken such measures."

"I did try to get your attention from offstage, when you were singing...but of course all your attention was on Christine. I should have known it would be, but I wanted to at least try."

"You did not try hard enough, Little Giry. You spent three years risking everything to write your notes and spy on me, and the moment where it counted the most, you decided to suddenly turn coward!" By now, Erik was directly in front of her, demanding every bit of her attention. "Where was your compassion then? Did you not care enough about Christine or myself to abandon your little game? No. You have absolutely no right to shed tears around me, Marguerite. You will never earn my pity." At this, Marguerite's sobs became louder, and she doubled over, clutching her stomach as if she had just been punched. Erik turned away from her then, refusing to care. *Let her think about her actions. Why should I care? Every time I do, it gets shoved back in my face.*

Curse you, Marguerite! Her sobs and wails had left her exhausted hours ago, and she had fallen asleep once more. But while Erik had been waiting eagerly for the silence to come over them once more, he hadn't once been able to take his mind off of Madame Giry. If his old friend hadn't survived, could he really place all the blame on Little Giry? He tried to think back to that night and what had been going through his mind. With a heavy sigh, he realized he had only been thinking about Christine and what could have been rather than the one who had saved his life. *Would Little Giry's word of warning really made a difference?* He looked over to the dancer, now too exhausted to be bothered by dreams and nightmares. The crust of bread had done nothing for her thinness, and at that moment, she shivered with no blanket to keep out the cold.

No! No mercy, no pity, and certainly no compassion! He turned away, fists clenched, while angry tears threatened to surface. He wondered what he would have done, had he received her warning. Would he have dared to show his face on stage then, even if it was his opera? He hated to think himself a coward, but the pain and humiliation from his childhood was still fresh in his mind. He recalled countless nights when he had dared to sleep. He remembered the dreams that had caused him to wake up in a pool of sweat and tears, with no one to comfort him and tell him it would be okay. No one to tell him it was only a dream, that it wasn't real. Instead, he was forced to look to himself for comfort, and so he would spend the rest of the night, singing or playing his violin, or listening to his music box over and over again.

But suppose he hadn't performed that night. Suppose he had let it go as rehearsed. *What a fool the Vicomte would have looked then!* He nearly laughed at the thought. *But what of Christine? She would have left shortly after the performance. And then what?* Would he have followed her to the ends of the earth if he had to? No. He would have found some way...some way...to bring her down here. *And she still would have resented you.* Her face appeared in his mind then, from when she had returned his ring. *It's over.* The angry tears turned to tears of sadness as they spilled out of his eyes. "Oh...Christine..." *Tell me it's not over...say that you love me...*

Erik spent the remainder of the day collapsed on the floor. Perhaps Marguerite awoke, perhaps not. He didn't notice and he didn't care. Just one look at Marguerite would once again remind him that Christine was long gone, and he needed no further reminder of that. His tears had dried, and he felt completely drained of all emotion and energy. He refused to sleep, however. Aside from Marguerite, sleep was his worst enemy at the moment. But he closed his red, swollen eyes anyway. He needed darkness. Perhaps he would die, here and now. The thought was quite comfortable. He imagined never having to open his eyes to the emptiness of his world, never having to be tortured by memories of Christine, never having to deal with another living soul. He could just wait here...wait for time to take its toll and nature to take its course. He would at last be free of all the pain that had held such control over his life. *Yes...death would be a beautiful song...*

He was in his mirror room, only he did not know the way out. Instead of twisting and rotating, the walls of mirrors seemed to be closing in around him. Instead of his own reflection, he saw only her. "Good bye, my Angel. It's over. Good bye..." Her words repeated themselves, growing louder and louder as her image got closer and closer. Behind her and beside her were images of small children, laughing and pointing. Just when the walls made contact with him, they all disappeared. In their place was Antoinette, surrounded by flames, and her scream shattered the mirrors around him.

Erik opened his eyes and immediately groaned. Sleep had defeated him once again, though he should have seen it coming. Grief would have been enough to overwhelm him with exhaustion, but now he had anger and confusion towards Marguerite on top of it all. For a moment, he considered setting her free to find her mother. *You'd like that, wouldn't you, Marguerite? To know that you've defeated me? Ha!* No, he would not give her the satisfaction. He rolled over to face her. She was still asleep, and for a moment, Erik felt a pang of jealousy towards her, for being able to sleep without nightmares. *Oh, no. If I am unable to sleep, why should she be allowed the luxury of it?* Besides, he still had questions.

Questions that she would answer should she ever hope to set foot into the light of day again.

Erik stood up, once again choosing to ignore the stiffness in his muscles and the dizziness from hunger. He would have enough to take his mind off of his weakness soon enough. Once at the dancer's side, he knelt down and began shaking her roughly. "Marguerite! Get up!" Her eyes fluttered open and immediately filled with confusion. Not waiting for her to get her bearings, Erik began pacing the floor.

"Good morning, Monsieur. Did you sleep well?"

"I'll be asking the questions here, insolent girl!" At his tone of voice, Marguerite shrunk back a little. "You will begin with answering as to how you reached the rooftop so quickly, let alone were able to leave a note for me."

"It was simple, really. I discovered that passageway quite some time ago. It was really only a matter of guessing that you would go there instead of down here."

"And the note? Surely you could not have found ink so quickly."

"From the first few notes on, I've always kept some scrap paper and a small piece of charcoal under my sashes and belts, just in case words came to mind when I was nowhere near the dorm rooms or my mother's quarters."

"I almost caught you that night. You should have known, especially after what happened to Buquet, how dangerous it would have been for you to follow me."

"It was a risk I was willing to take, Monsieur. I wanted to know that what you did was appreciated. It was not exactly what I'd had in mind, but to be sure you took care of our problem in your own way. When I got there, I saw you hiding from Christine and Raoul...I was watching your face the entire time. It broke my heart..."

"Yes, I read that, Little Giry." Erik sighed, rubbing his hands through his thin hair in frustration. So many times those words had repeated themselves in his mind, and they were just as puzzling now. How could anyone, save for Christine, dare to say those words to him, unless they meant it as a joke? *Pity at most. Nothing more. It has to be.*

"Then tell me, Monsieur, why are you so angry when all I did was care? Is there no room in your heart for a friend?"

"I have no need nor desire for pity, Mademoiselle! I did not ask you for pity nor help! Instead, I asked you to leave me alone, and yet you still insisted on interfering! Why should I not be angry?"

"Monsieur, don't you understand? I do not pity you! Not once did I use that word! You can take care of yourself, to be sure. Is it so hard to believe that someone other than Christine or my mother would care about you?"

"If you truly cared about me, Little Giry, you would never have tried to stand in my way."

"They were notes. Bits of scrap paper. They could hardly stand in your way."

"How quickly you forget, Marguerite! It was not a mere message that called out to me in the stables! Explain that to me!"

"I was following Christine that night. I saw her face...I had never seen it so fragile...so vulnerable..."

"I saw how fragile she was. What were you doing awake so early, that you knew Christine was going anywhere?"

"Something else I inherited from my mother, I suppose...I've been waking up early with her for as long as I can remember. I suppose we find the early morning hours quiet and peaceful, and it's the only time we have for just the two of us...I was going to her quarters when I saw Christine."

"So you had no knowledge of me being there? How, then, did you expect to protect her, should the need have presented itself?"

"I don't know what I was thinking...perhaps I just wanted to talk to her...but then I saw you in the shadows..."

"You must have been looking hard..." Erik refused to think that his hiding spot had been that obvious. "Besides, Marguerite, you should have known by then that I would never have harmed her."

"True enough, Monsieur, but you were going to harm the carriage driver."

"Only a little..." Erik shifted uncomfortably, trying unsuccessfully to hide a smirk. "However, once again, Little Giry, you failed to look at the situation from my perspective."

"What would you have done when you got there, Monsieur? More deception? More false comfort and lies?"

"Let me make one thing clear, Mademoiselle Giry. If there was anything about me that wasn't a mask, it was my comfort for Christine! I know firsthand the pain that she felt! You call yourself her friend, yet it was I who found her in the chapel, crying out to a father who was not there! It was *my* voice she heard! It was *I* who shaped her voice into what it is! I have always, *always* been there to hear her painful, lonely cries, and the one time I could have been real to her...the one time she could have cried on my shoulder, you took it from me! Because of you, Christine is probably miles away from Paris by now, and you have lost your friend. You had no right trying to talk her into staying, when it is you who pushed her away!"

"You saw that?" Marguerite bit her lip, lowering her gaze to the floor.

"Of course I did, Little Giry, or have you also forgotten that this is my theater!"

"Oh yes...how can I forget, you're the Phantom of the Opera."

"I *was*." Erik turned away, glancing down.

"Please, Monsieur...if you are not the Opera Ghost or the Phantom of the Opera, who are you?"

"That is enough questions for today. Go back to sleep if you wish. Just leave me alone." *You are not getting that last piece of me, Little Giry. Not that easily!*

Chapter 9: Regarding Antoinette

"Marguerite,

In order to ease both our minds, I have decided to go upstairs and see if I might find your mother. Wait here. You are not to touch anything."

Erik left the unsigned note next to the sleeping dancer, and with no further hesitation, he slipped through the doorway. Making his way through the caverns, he attempted time and time again to erase the memory of the recurring nightmare. Yet, try his might, he could not escape from the echoes of Antoinette's screams and the shattering mirrors. He had once again let himself drift into sleep, and once again, the mirror dream had come to him. Of all the things that could drive him to madness, finding Antoinette was the one matter he could easily take care of. Yes, the sooner he found her, the sooner the nightmares would disappear.

As he stepped through the mirror into his living quarters, he stopped. Images of Christine were everywhere. The mob hadn't completely destroyed his home, and he wasn't sure if he was grateful or not. A flood of memories came rushing to him now, and he nearly collapsed. *She's been here...her touch is everywhere...* A familiar tingle came to his lips, only this time there was a bitter aftertaste. *She rejected you...she betrayed you...she still has your heart...* Tears came to his eyes, but he forced them back. He needed to focus on finding Antoinette. The wound that Christine had left on him was still fresh...to pick at it now would surely drive him into madness right then and there.

He waded through the lake water, remembering only that which aided in reaching the upstairs passageways. He had no fear of running into anyone; surely the fire and resulting damage would have discouraged any further search parties. He was counting on the theory that just having Christine back with them would have satisfied them enough. *She is precious to all of us...*

Upon reaching the top of the stairs, he contemplated where to start. He closed his eyes, painfully recalling the night of his opera. Antoinette had watched the entire show from off-stage... he vaguely recalled seeing a glimpse of her face once she realized who he was... she'd been the first to recognize him. But surely she couldn't have stayed there through the chandelier crash...*where could she have gone?*

Raoul. He certainly could not have found his way down to Erik's caverns without help. Antoinette had told him about your past...surely he would have turned to her for help that night. But she couldn't have gone very far. Raoul had come alone, and Madame Giry had always been uneasy about Erik's darkness. Erik looked around then. This was the most likely passageway she would have chosen. Nodding, he pressed on down the corridor, checking through every peephole and taking in the damage. The fire had spread quickly, it seemed, and he quickened his pace. *Where are you?* His nightmares were one thing. Seeing the reality of the damage he had caused, he was now faced with genuine concern for the ballet instructor. *She saved your life once. You could not have saved hers in return?*

    At last, he reached the end of the corridor, and he peered into the dorm room through one of the vents. Relief swept over him then. *She's alive.* Yes, there she was, standing among the rubble and burnt furniture. In the dim light, he could see ribbons of tears on her face, and he immediately recognized the signs of lack of sleep and nourishment. *What have you done to yourself, Antoinette?* He forced himself to remain silent, however, for she appeared to be saying something. "Oh, my daughter, where have you gone? Marguerite..." The pain on her face matched the pain he was feeling for Christine, and he clutched his chest. *You should ease her mind.*

But he wasn't ready to set Marguerite free just yet. She would learn her lesson, no matter how long it took. He needed to do something for Antoinette, however. She deserved peace of mind. Slowly, Erik moved his face as close to the vent as he dared. "She's safe, Antoinette. Do not worry about her any longer." He watched as she looked around, confusion drying her tears for only a moment.

"Who is there?" She called out, but Erik was already halfway down the corridor. He couldn't bear it any longer; his own pain was enough to deal with. Descending the stairs, he wondered whether he should take the boat. Leaving it on this side of the lake would be like leaving a door wide open into his caverns. Yet the lake was shallow enough; one boat would make no difference. Besides, he needed a good long swim.

He reached the banks of his living quarters a good hour later, cold water dripping off of him. *Oh, how I needed that!* He knew the relief would be only temporary, but at the moment, it was worth it. He had peeled off his clothes mid-swim, freeing himself of the last visual connection to 'Don Juan' and Christine's betrayal. Quickly drying off, he changed into his regular suit of dark clothes. At the last moment, he grabbed his cape. He did not plan on wearing it, however. If he had told Antoinette that

Marguerite was safe, he would make sure that she was, even if it was only against the cold.

Lastly, he gathered the rest of his food storage and caught a few fish in the lake before wrapping everything up in the cape. As an afterthought, he also grabbed a couple extra candles. Not wanting to linger among his memories any longer, he stepped back through the mirror. As he approached the hidden doorway, he hesitated once more. Had he imagined it? No, there was no mistaking the sound for anything else. Marguerite was singing.

It was not an aimless tune, either. She was singing 'Think of Me'. *Christine's song.* Curiosity shattered, Erik stormed into the room. She stopped singing as soon as she saw him, greeting him with a cheerful smile that melted away a good portion of his anger. "Did you find her, Monsieur?" Her brown eyes were wide and bright, filled with nothing but hope.

"She's alive. I told her you're safe." Erik moved past her and busied himself with feeding the fire.

"I suppose that means I'm not free yet." The dancer sighed. Erik remained silent. *You have your answers, Erik. What's stopping you?* Pride, he supposed. To free her now, having not punished her to his satisfaction, would be admitting defeat. *So was letting Christine go.* Silently shouting curses at his doubtful thoughts, he unwrapped the bundle he had brought from his caverns and placed its contents into the food storage under the table. He saved out the fish, however, and retrieved a dagger from the food pit before replacing the stones. Standing, he flung the fish at Marguerite.

"I want these cleaned and cooked thoroughly. If it's not done perfectly, you do not get this cape." Until he could figure out a plan, he would make sure that she earned her keep.

Apparently, she's been taking lessons from Paulette. Erik concluded as he finished his portion of the fish. True to his word, he threw the cape to the dancer. "You'll want to wash that, unless you enjoy smelling of dead fish." Marguerite nodded, silently taking the garment over to the pool. "Clean the dagger as well." Erik suppressed a smirk as she retraced her steps. "And when you're done with that, you will scrub the floor of that mess you made with the fish."

"Yes, Monsieur." Marguerite's words were few and polite, but Erik could sense a trace of impatience on her face. *Is this what you want? To drive her mad and then set her free? What will Antoinette think?* His old friend's face came into his mind, a distant look on her pale, thin face. *No! I thought I was rid of this torture!*

As the next few days passed, Erik mentally weighed the situation. Marguerite seemed to be coping with whatever he threw at her. Antoinette was sick with worry. He had never seen mother and daughter away from each other until the night of the fire. He would have expected that by now, Marguerite would be showing some sign of fear of him, but she was much stronger than he'd thought. Her tears seemed to have dried up long ago, as soon as she'd heard that her mother was alive. This new hope seemed to shield her from him. The more time that passed, the more he came to realize that no matter how much her notes had angered him, Christine's parting had weakened him to the point where he could not bring himself to break his prisoner. He needed time alone, and Antoinette needed her daughter. Because of Erik, she had lost everything. *Why would you make her pay for the sins which are Marguerite's?*

With a sigh, Erik looked over to where Marguerite was scrubbing the floor, humming a small tune. Purely out of habit, he spoke up in anger. "Did I ask you to sing, Little Giry? You are not Christine."

"I know I'm not, Monsieur... I just grow tired of the silence, is all. Singing helps to take my mind off of my mother." Marguerite looked down at the floor. *So if I ask you to stop singing, your fortress will crumble.* But no...the music was somehow soothing to him, even if it wasn't Christine. After all, Marguerite was no Carlotta either.

"Is it not enough to know that she is alive, Little Giry?"

"No, it's not, Monsieur... I just want to see her...one last time...just to say good bye, and then I will do whatever you ask of me. I promise."

"You would...sacrifice everything...your mother's happiness...*your* happiness...for me?" He hadn't shed tears in so long, building a mask of anger and indifference to keep Marguerite at a distance. But her words just now began to destroy that shell, and he forced himself to turn away.

"Monsieur, think of it. Even though I am not here entirely willingly, where would you be if I was not with you? Your fever from those first few days...it could have killed you, Monsieur. And I know you try to hide it, but I see those unshed tears. I see the pain in your eyes. You must grieve for as long as it takes. Your pain may last a lifetime, and I am prepared to stand by your side and take care of you until that time comes."

"You can do nothing for me. Only Christine..." He couldn't fight the tears any longer, and they came pouring out of his eyes. He felt her hand on his shoulder, but he was too exhausted to shake it off.

"I know I'm not Christine, Monsieur, and I'm not trying to be. Consider me no more than a helping hand and a listening ear." Her hand moved across the back of his shoulders, and he felt her pull him into her. Childlike instinct took over then, and he leaned into her, turning to cry on her shoulder. *Everything will be okay.*

The next day, Erik led Marguerite through the hidden doorway. No words were spoken on the journey through the passageways and to the upstairs. She did not complain about wading through the lake, and her face remained expressionless until they reached the end of the upstairs corridor. Just as before, Antoinette was standing in the middle of the room, only her face seemed much paler and thinner. Marguerite did not cry out until the secret doorway was opened, and even then, both mother and daughter stared at each other as if in a dream. "As I said, Antoinette, your daughter is safe." Erik broke the silence, gently pushing the dancer forward.

"Marguerite..." Antoinette stepped forward to embrace her daughter. Instead of a emotional reunion, however, Erik watched as Madame Giry went limp, and Marguerite screamed. Erik rushed forward and grabbed the ballet instructor. Turning her over, he lowered her to the floor.

"She's all right, Marguerite. Merely fainted. I'll need to bring her down to the caverns until she is well."

"I'll help." The dancer wiped her tears away. Erik got to his feet and carried his friend back down through the passageways, Marguerite's footsteps close behind. Once they reached his living quarters, he quickly brought Antoinette to his bed.

"Marguerite, wait here. I need to fetch some food from the other room. Put a damp cloth on her head while I'm gone."

"Yes, Monsieur."

"Erik."

"What?"

"You may call me Erik, Meg." Leaving Meg to her thoughts, he quickly proceeded down the secret passageway once more.

Chapter 10: More Changes

"Has there been any change?" Erik placed the food on a nearby table and approached the bed. Meg looked up at him, tears in her eyes. Her hand remained on the damp cloth, and she continued to softly move it across her mother's face.

"No, nothing..."

"Perhaps now that she's seen you, she's getting the sleep she needs. She'll be all right, Meg."

"I hope so, Erik...I've just never seen her so weak..." Meg turned her face back to Antoinette.

"I can recall one other time. You were too young to remember. It was after your father died. She didn't leave her quarters for weeks after that."

"Of course. I was only three at the time."

"But she recovered then, and she'll recover now. She just needs a bit of rest, as do you."

"You need it more, Erik. I haven't seen you sleep in days."

"I... I'll be fine." Erik turned away.

"Is it the nightmares?" She was standing next to him now. *Is she a mind reader now?* He did not answer, and she continued. "Please. Get some sleep, Erik. If the nightmares wake you, I'll be here."

"It's not wise for you to order me around."

"I don't care. You need sleep. I'll not watch you die of exhaustion."

"Fine. I'll be down the secret passageway behind the broken mirror. But if anything changes, you will fetch me immediately. Third stone from the left corner, sixth one down."

"I promise I'll notify you of any changes." With nothing left to say, Erik turned and stepped into the dark corridor. He would not have given in so easily, but he was too exhausted to argue. *Curses. She's right again.* He had no sooner reached the blankets beside the fireplace before he collapsed into a deep sleep.

"Erik! Erik!" Someone was shaking him. And whoever it was had better have a very good reason or a written will prepared. Opening his eyes, he saw that it was Meg. Groaning, he turned over so his back was to her. For once, he hadn't had any nightmares, and now his sleep was being interrupted. "Erik, it's Mama. She's awake." That did it. Fully awake, Erik slowly got to his feet.

"Has she said anything?"

"Only asked where she was and where you were. I gave her a bit of bread and some water."

"Good. That's good." Erik rubbed his forehead.

"I'm sorry, Erik. Just tell me what to do, and then you can go back to sleep."

"No, it's useless now, Meg. I'm awake now." Erik stumbled over to the pool and doused his head in the cool water. "Come. It would not be wise to leave her alone very long." With that, the two made their way back to where Antoinette was sitting up on the bed, nibbling on the bread while looking around, puzzled. As soon as she saw him, she lowered the bread to her lap.

"Erik..."

"There will be plenty of time for questions later, Antoinette. What you need now is to fully recover, for your daughter's sake."

"Meg..." Antoinette reached out her hand, and Meg took it, sitting back down on the bed beside her.

"Yes, I'm here, Mama. We're all safe now."

"You could do with a bit of sleep yourself, Meg. It's been a trying day." Erik pointed out.

"Will you be alright, Erik?" Meg looked at him with those big brown eyes, and he felt something shift inside him.

"I'll be fine." Erik gave her a half-smile, and that seemed to be enough for the dancer. Mother and daughter were soon fast asleep. Erik looked around the caverns. *This place is a mess.* Broken glass and music sheets were everywhere, and more than half of the candles needed to be replaced; they were nothing but tiny stubs of melted wax. Slowly, he bent down to pick up a solitary page. It was a long-forgotten song he had written for Christine, from the beginning of her lessons. *I can't do this...I can't say good bye.* Collapsing to the floor, he lost himself in his loud, carefree sobs. Only when he felt a hand lightly touch his arm did he look up. Slowly, Meg reached up to his face and brushed at his tears with the back of her hand. "I thought I told you to go to sleep." Erik sniffed.

"And I told you that I'm here for you, didn't I?" Meg matched his stubborn tone. Tears outweighing his pride at the moment, Erik buried his head in her shoulder. As he wept, he felt her lightly move her hand across his forehead and rub his shoulder, all while softly humming a tune he did not recognize. It didn't matter. It was soothing, and he needed to focus on something other than the piece of his past he still held in his hand. He closed his eyes, drinking in the music until his tears slowed to a small trickle. Her hand returned to his face, brushing at the remaining tears. Slowly, he brought his own hand up to stop the soothing motion. Opening his eyes, he met her gaze.

"It's no use, Meg. I love Christine...I need her...I feel my very life seeping out of me without her..."

"You mustn't talk like that, Erik...I won't let you die."

"Then you must find her for me, Meg. I shouldn't have let her go...I'm not ready to say good bye..." He felt himself start to sweat, and his head began to spin. He closed his eyes once more, and the last thing he remembered before sleep overtook him was Meg lowering him to the cold stone floor.

Distant voices. "How is he, Meg?"

"No change. He still asks for her."

"We must get him out of this damp air."

"I know the way out. I'll fetch the doctor." The tiny hand on his forehead left. *Christine...*

A familiar tune. Erik opened his eyes and immediately saw his music box on the bedside table. Across the room, Meg was sitting on a window seat, peering outside. *Where am I?* As he struggled to sit up, Meg turned her head, and he saw that she'd been crying.

"Oh..Erik! I'm so relieved!" In just a few steps, she was at his side once more.

"Why did you take me out of my caverns? I was safe there..."

"You were dying there, Erik. This was the only way... I had to fetch the doctor. He brought you to his house... there's more privacy here than in the hospital."

"How long was I..."

"Several weeks. I was so scared...I thought we had lost you."

"Would that have really been so terrible? What good am I to you?"

"You saved my mother's life. And your music...it would be wrong for your music to go unshared." She looked down, seeming to be holding something back. He did not pursue it, however. He was still dizzy.

"How is your mother?"

"She has fully recovered, thanks to you. You were right. All she needed was a good rest." At that moment, the bedroom door opened. Antoinette appeared, holding a steaming mug in her hand. "Mama! Erik's awake!" Meg exclaimed.

"Oh good. I brought you some soup, but perhaps you could feed it to Erik instead. I will bring you some more."

"Of course." Meg took the mug from her and returned to the bed.

"Before I taste a drop of that, Meg...there is no point in my eating anything unless you can tell me that you've found Christine."

"Please, Erik...I've already almost lost you twice now. Please don't make me go through that again."

"Tell me the truth, Meg. Did you find her or not?"

"It does not matter if I did nor not. She won't see you." Meg looked away, tears beginning to fall once more. "Don't ask me to tell you any more than that. It will only send you right back into a feverish state." *So she did find her. It's a start. Something was obviously wrong, however.*

"Just give me the soup, Meg. You did what I asked you to." *I'll find out everything I need to know one way or another.*

Chapter 11: Finding Christine

Erik collapsed onto the window seat, thoroughly drained. Exhausted or not, he was unaccustomed to staying in bed all day. Resting his head on the wall behind him, he peered out the window at the streets of Paris below. This was what he was used to. He had grown used to watching people while remaining hidden to the point where he thoroughly enjoyed it. Yes, even now, he watched several children chasing each other among peddlers and couples walking hand in hand. A sharp pain surged through his chest at the sight of all the lovers below, and for a moment he envisioned one of the pairs as himself and Christine. *Perhaps in another life...with another face...* He sighed, and a single tear made its way down his cheek.

He turned his attention to the buildings around him. Down the street stood a massive building that looked all too familiar. Yet how strange it was to see the opera house looking so rundown...so empty. He had to admit it was fortunate that the doctor lived so close; any further and there would have been no way to avoid drawing attention to his disfigurement. Yet he also found it torturous to be so close and yet so far from his home and his music. His hands were growing restless. He needed something to occupy his time.

As he was pondering this, the door swung open. "Erik, for goodness sake, get back into bed!" *Antoinette. Always the worrier.* Erik managed a smirk and turned to face her.

"I'm fine, Antoinette. Merely bored is all."

"Nonsense. Your face is still pale and shows your exhaustion. Now if you refuse to return to bed on your own, I will be forced to fetch the doctor."

"Antoinette, are you threatening me?" Erik raised an eyebrow.

"Suppose I am? What can you do about it? You can barely walk without collapsing from dizziness." Antoinette motioned for him to stand. Erik reluctantly did so, refusing Antoinette's helping hand as he made his way back to the bed. "And if you're really all that bored, Erik, Meg was sure to bring over your violin and a stack of blank paper." Madame Giry pointed to where the instrument stood in the far corner. Erik merely nodded, and the violin was brought over to him. "The paper is on the bedside table, as well as plenty of ink." But Erik wasn't paying attention. As he ran his hand across the smooth wood, bitterness rose up inside him. *How can I even think of playing music without Christine to hear it?* But if and when he found her, wouldn't he want to have a new song to play for her? Slowly, he picked up the bow and positioned the violin under his chin. "Before I leave you to your music, Erik, there's something I must know. What was my daughter doing down in your caverns that night?"

"You mean she didn't tell you?" Erik lowered the bow and looked up at her. When the ballet instructor shook her head, Erik sighed and lifted his bow once more. "Why don't you ask her? Ask her about the notes. And don't let her go until she tells you the entire truth." With that, he began testing the notes and tuning the strings.

"How could you?" Meg stormed into the room hours later. Erik opened his eyes, reluctantly placing the violin aside. *Something tells me she's going to be here for awhile.*

"How could I what?" He had a good idea as to what she was talking about, but he decided to play with her a little bit. *After all, she played around with me first.*

"You know very well what! How could you tell her about the notes? They were private!"

"If they were so private, Little Giry, you would have kept them to yourself."

"We've been over this before, Erik. I couldn't keep them to myself. They were my way of being heard."

"Then you have nothing to be angry about. As soon as you gave those notes to me, they became mine to do as I please."

"Of course I have a right to be angry! Telling my mother about the notes was like Christine ripping the mask off your face! You betrayed my secret!" By now, tears were streaming down her red face, and she made no attempt to wipe them away.

"That's where you're wrong, Marguerite! There's a world of difference!"

"Really? Name one thing that was different!"

"Simple. Your notes were just a game. My secret was a necessity to my very survival."

"If you think it was all just a game, Erik, then you must not have really read them. You haven't heard a single word I've said." Her tone was cold, and as the tears took over, she ran out of the room. Alone once more, Erik returned to his violin music while his thoughts replayed the conversation. *Perhaps the notes had been more than a game to her.*

But can she really compare her notes to my masks and darkness? She had no reason to hide. Her face was far from being deformed, and she'd said herself that she did not fear him. What, then, had she feared? To be sure, the note regarding Joseph Buquet should have been anonymous, as the stagehand had his own way of sneaking around the opera house. *But what of the others?* Sighing, he resolved to question her further upon her next visit.

Over the next several days, Erik was forced to do nothing but recover, as the three meals a day caused him to gain back his strength in no time. *At least now I can search for Christine.* Meg was obviously not going to tell him anything about the soprano's whereabouts, and any questions on his part would only lead to more silence. Besides, she had been avoiding him ever since that heated conversation, and so he had never gotten a chance to pursue an answer to his questions. *No matter.* His song was finished, ready for Christine's ears. There was nothing keeping him here. And so, in the dead of night, he gathered up his violin and his music sheets before silently making his way down the stairs and out the back door. He left behind his music box, but no note. *Why should I give them opportunity to stop me?*

As he walked through the streets of Paris, he kept to the shadows while pondering where to begin. To be sure, the Vicomte was well-known enough that anyone would be able to direct him to Roaul's estate, but he was reluctant to draw any attention to himself. However, he did want to put as much distance as possible between himself and the Giry women. He decided that the best option would be to move beyond the city limits. Had Christine not said that she would be leaving Paris anyway?

He decided to begin at the opera house. His visit would be quick enough; he just wanted to see if the managers' offices had survived, and if so, if there was any address or other indication as to where their precious patron resided.

He quickened his pace as he approached familiar surroundings. Stepping inside the burnt opera house, he easily found the offices, still intact. He set the violin down and began searching the papers cluttering up the desk. He didn't have to look very long. Near the top of one stack was an envelope with the de Chagny address clearly written on it. *Perfect.* Grabbing the envelope, he retrieved his violin and hurried out of the opera house. Glancing back at the doctor's house, he noticed a single candle moving around his former room. Meg's face appeared for only a moment, and from the shadows, Erik saw the worried expression in her eyes. *No regrets. I'll burden them no longer.* Turning away, he began his journey.

The Vicomte's estate was easy enough to find, and as it came into view, the bitterness in Erik's mouth was so strong that he felt as though he would be sick. *It's a show of his wealth, nothing more. You deserve much more, Christine!* It was just before dawn, and all the windows were still dark. *No matter. I'm here now. There's no hurry.* Spotting a fairly large group of bushes near the back of the house, Erik decided it would make a good hiding spot. He had no sooner made himself comfortable when he felt his eyelids grow heavy. Satisfied that he was once more close to his love, he surrendered to a deep sleep.

Three hours later, he awoke with a shiver to find a small bird perched on one of the branches, staring at him and chirping. As soon as Erik shifted position, the bird flew away. *Go ahead. Leave me. Everyone else does.* He then remembered where he was. *Christine.* Slowly, he stood up to study the windows on this side of the mansion. The closest room appeared to be the dining room, and he nearly collapsed all over again. Christine was seated at the table, along with the de Chagnys. They were apparently in the middle of breakfast, so deep in their conversation that they paid no attention to the window. Erik wasn't about to take any chances, however. Retrieving his violin from the bushes, he walked around the house, finally choosing a balcony that was right by a tree. Effortlessly, he made his way up the trunk and over the balcony railing. Peering through the glass door, he noticed a familiar hairbrush on the vanity. *Christine.* He placed himself on the balcony where the inside curtains would keep him hidden until he was ready.

He didn't have to wait very long. Just as he was finishing reading over the song, he heard voices from inside. "Your bath is ready for you, Mademoiselle Daae, but you must hurry." A maid, obviously.

"Thank you, Adelaide.. I just can't believe it. Today I become Vicomtess..." Erik could hear the grin in her voice, and that sick feeling returned. *Not if I can help it.*

"I'll leave you to your bath now. Your dress will be on the bed waiting for you."

"Thank you, Adelaide. And if you see the Giry's arrive, you may send them right up." The maid did not respond, but Erik could hear the door close. Wasting no time, he placed the violin into position and began playing the song. Within moments, just as expected, the glass doors were opened, and out stepped Christine. Her eyes had that ever so familiar trance-like look to them, and as he sang, she closed the distance between them. Standing in front of her, Erik set the violin aside.

"You still love me, Christine. Otherwise you would not have come to me. My music...my heart...is still yours. It always will be."

"My Angel..." Christine whispered.

"Christine! No!" Out of nowhere, Raoul rushed out onto the balcony and grasped his fiancé.

"Raoul..." Christine blinked, seeming to be waking up from a dream.

"Go back inside. I'll take care of this." Christine merely nodded, and without glancing back, she went back into her room.

"You order her around as if she were a mere servant? Oh yes, that really shows how much you love her." Erik scoffed. The Vicomte responded with his fists, and when Erik grabbed onto his wrists, Raoul kicked him in the stomach. Doubled over, Erik could do nothing but let a second kick knock him to the floor. The Vicomte was soon on top of him, and blow after blow made contact with Erik's already bloody and bruised face. To be sure, Erik landed quite a few punches of his own, but the kick to the stomach had weakened him by far. Just when the Vicomte was raising his fist once more, sure to land a blow that would end it all, a familiar voice cried out.

"No, Raoul! Leave him alone!" Right before Erik blanked out, he felt the Vicomte get up off of him, and he saw Meg's blurry figure rushing to his side.

"Erik? Erik, please wake up...don't leave..." Erik slowly opened his swollen eyes and shivered. Cold damp cloths seemed to be covering every inch of him.

"Christine..." He managed, closing his hand around the one that had been on his wrist.

"No...it's me, Meg. Christine is downstairs." He heard Meg sniffle.

"Christine..."

"Let me get something for those eyes." He felt her pull away, and he struggled to sit up. As pain roared through his body, he was forced to lay back down on the bed. "You mustn't move around, Erik. The doctor thinks you've broken a rib."

"Doctor...?" His head was beginning to ache, and he felt her place an ice cold cloth over his eyes.

"Yes...the de Chagnys are letting you stay here overnight. The doctor will be taking you back to his house first thing in the morning."

"No...need to see Christine..."

"I'm sorry, Erik." Her voice was shaky, and he felt her hands moving through his hair. The motion was comforting to him, and he leaned into her touch. "I need to rub some ointment on your cuts and bruises. Don't be alarmed." *Why would I be alarmed? Stinging ointment is the least of my concerns.* One by one, the cloths were lifted, and as soon as the ointment was applied to each section of his skin, the cloth was replaced. Slowly, relief came to his face, his shoulders, his chest, and his stomach. Just then, he felt her lift a cloth from his upper leg, and he instinctively grasped her hand to stop her. "Your leg is bruised just as much as the rest of you, Erik. It's just your leg. Everything else is still covered up."

"Leave it." *I can deal with the pain.*

"Suit yourself." The cloth was replaced, and an awkward silence fell over them. Chills ran up and down Erik's body, and he shivered.

"Am I unworthy of a de Chagny blanket?" He finally questioned, bitter sarcasm dripping from his voice.

"I had to remove it in order to care for your bruises. Here..." Warmth fell over him as the blanket was returned, and the shivers stopped. "Would you like anything? Water, perhaps? Warm broth?" *I only want Christine.* But he knew the answer to that.

"Why are you here?"

"The doctor is busy making arrangements for you, and everyone else has other things on their mind." She was hiding something again, and this time, he wasn't about to leave it alone.

"No...why are you here and not back in Paris? You could not have followed me..."

"I...I came for the wedding..." He heard her sigh as she sat down on the bed next to him.

"And when were you planning on telling me this? When you got back?" Anger rose up inside him once more; only the pain kept him from leaping to his feet.

"I'm so sorry, Erik...please...you're not strong enough...I shouldn't have told you..." Now you fear me. "Please...forget I said anything. You need your rest." Her hand returned to his forehead. As her fingers moved through his hair, he felt himself relax as sleep won over once again.

Chapter 12: Helpless

"We must be reasonable about this, Madame Giry." Raoul's voice broke through the silence. Now awake and alert, Erik kept his eyes closed underneath the cold cloths. From what he could hear, it seemed as though quite a few people had entered his room.

"I am being perfectly reasonable, Monsieur. Look at him. He cannot even move a muscle, and you wish to send him to jail?"

"He brought this on himself, Madame Giry. Have you forgotten the murders? The fire? Not to mention we had to delay the wedding because of him."

"He left me in charge of his money, Raoul. I'm sure it will cover all the damages. As for him coming here...I think you've done enough to make things even."

"I cannot in good conscience allow you to set him free. How can you be sure that he won't try this again?" There was a slight hesitation, and the Vicomte continued. "There, you see? You can't be sure. I told you before that he has turned to madness. You're just too close to him that you can't see it."

"No...please...there must be another way..." Meg's voice now, and Erik felt her hand on his shoulder.

"There is, Meg. Do not worry. Your father has a brother who lives far away in the country. We will go there."

"It doesn't matter how far away you send him. He found us once, he'll find us again. Think of Christine." *She's fragile...precious to all of us...I would never harm her...*

"If he finds you again, Vicomte, I cannot stop you from sending for the police. But right now, until he is fully healed, he is in my care." Erik pictured Madame Giry staring the young Vicomte down; he was sorry that he wasn't able to see it.

"Very well. His actions are on your shoulders. Now get him out of my sight." Retreating footsteps followed the Vicomte's statement, and Erik inwardly smirked at the defeated tone in his voice. He felt Meg gently squeeze his shoulder, as if she was aware that he was awake.

"Come, Meg...we must help Christine get ready for the wedding, and the doctor needs space to get Erik ready for the journey back."

"Before you go, Madame Giry..." The doctor's voice sounded then, "I will need some assistance on the journey to Paris. The carriage ride is sure to be a bumpy one, and I will need someone to keep Erik steady."

"I'll go." Meg volunteered.

"And have you miss this important day in Christine's life? I cannot allow it, Meg."

"She knows I'm happy for the both of them, Mama. She needs you here more...you've been like a mother to her."

"Very well. At least come with me now. The doctor will let you know when he's ready." With that, the hand on his shoulder left him, and two sets of footsteps left the room.

Despite the bumps in the road, Erik dozed for most of the journey back, even though he couldn't ignore the constant feeling of Meg's arms on either side of his torso. *Why would you sacrifice your friend's happiness for me?* His thoughts would then turn to Christine, walking down the aisle and further away from him. He refused to think of the possibility that he would never see her again. *Someday, somehow, I will find you. You still need me.*

The carriage slowed to a stop just before noon. "Wait here," he heard the doctor say to Meg. "While I fetch some bandages, I need you to check on his eyes and uncover his torso."

"Yes, Monsieur." Meg responded, and moments later, Erik felt the cloths over his eyes being removed. "Erik? Are you awake?"

"Awake enough." Erik replied, and he slowly opened his eyes.

"The swelling's gone down." Meg observed before reaching for the cloths on his torso.

Erik reached for her hand, stopping the motion. "Why didn't you stay? I thought you care about Christine's happiness." She did not look at him, nor did she reply. Finally realizing that she wasn't going to answer, Erik released her hand and sighed. Just then, the doctor returned with a large roll of thick material.

"Mademoiselle, I need you to wrap this around him while I hold him up. Wrap it tight, but not so much that he won't be able to breathe."

"Yes, Monsieur." As Meg took the bandages from the doctor, Erik kept his eyes on her while he felt the doctor's arms on his back. Slowly, he was lifted into a sitting position, but the doctor was able to keep his back straight while Meg wrapped the seemingly endless roll of material around him.

Finally, the bandage was on, and Erik waited to be set back down. Instead, the doctor kept him in position.

"Very well done. You would make an excellent nurse, should you ever desire it."

"Thank you, Monsieur, but I would rather stick to dancing."

"Then perhaps sometime you could dance for the patients at the hospital. I'm sure they would enjoy it."

"I'll think about it." Meg flashed a polite smile at the doctor, but Erik could see uncertainty in her eyes.

"Excellent. Now, if you would grasp his legs, I have a chair set up outside the carriage." Chair? Eyes wide open now, Erik was helpless as he was slowly moved out of the carriage and into the sunlight. His eyes automatically squinted; never before had he been out in the noonday sun. Never. Even in the fair, he mostly kept to the tents, either willingly or not. As his eyes adjusted, his gaze immediately fell on a wooden chair in front of him.

"What on earth is that contraption?" He questioned.

"Monsieur, it is just a common wheelchair. Surely you don't expect us to carry you?" The doctor replied from behind him.

"There's still the stairs." Erik pointed.

"No stairs. Not this time. My wife is setting up a room downstairs for your use." With that, Erik was placed in the chair, and the doctor wheeled him up a small ramp and into the house. "Wait here. I'll go see if your room is ready." As soon as he disappeared down the corridor, Erik turned to Meg.

"Good. He's gone. Get me out of this thing."

"Erik, this is not the time to be stubborn. You know perfectly well that you can't walk." Seeming to notice the helplessness in Erik's face, she softened her tone. "I know it's hard depending on all of us when you've been on your own for so long. But this is only temporary." She moved her hand through his hair, and once again, Erik found himself leaning into her touch. *I really shouldn't get used to this. She's not Christine.* "Shall I get your music box? It's still upstairs..." *Yes...music will be good...* Erik merely nodded in reply, and Meg bounced up the stairs. Alone once more, listening to the doctor and his wife converse, Erik succumbed to the tears that had been building up inside him. *Curse you, Vicomte, for leaving me helpless but not dead!*

Once Erik was settled in, the doctor left his wife in charge while he brought the carriage back to the de Chagny estate. "I will be back in the morning with Madame Giry." He promised. Erik once again asked Meg if she wanted to go with him, but the young dancer claimed she was too exhausted. Erik studied her face for several minutes then. While he had to admit that she did look fatigued, he had a feeling that she wasn't telling the whole truth. There was no chance to pursue it, however, as the doctor's wife sent Meg straight up to bed with a tray of lunch.

"None for me. I'm not hungry," Erik told Lucille when she offered him his own lunch.

"Ah...you're tired as well?" Erik didn't respond, but Lucille continued anyway. "Just as well, I suppose. My husband told me that you'll be needing plenty of rest. Just call me if you need anything." Erik simply nodded, and he was once again left alone. Winding up the music box, he let the familiar tune lull him to sleep.

Over the next several days, Meg gradually stepped into the role of Erik's caregiver. She still kept her distance, however, shadowing the doctor or Lucille while they did most of the hands-on work. Every chance Erik got, he studied her face, trying to make eye contact so she could see the unspoken questions in his face. *Eventually you will have to talk to me.* Her actions seemed very strange to him; up until they had left the opera house, her notes and her presence during his heartbreak had proved her to be an admirer to the point of being a complete nuisance. *What changed?*

Perhaps it was all a trick; her trying to get him to be the pursuer. *If that's the case, your attempt is futile. I will never feel for anyone the way I felt for Christine.* Whatever her reasons were, he could feel himself going mad all over again. *What is this hold she has over me?* The more he thought about it, the more he felt the anger returning. He thought of asking Antoinette to force it out of her, but he refused to let his old friend think that he was even a tiny bit interested in her daughter. *Which I'm not.*

And so, in the many moments that he was alone, he would play his violin aimlessly, while behind closed eyes he would erase time and past events in his mind. How he longed to go back to all those nights singing with Christine in the chapel, before the notes started, before she saw under his mask, before Raoul. "Oh, Christine...why?" He would ask the darkness. *Is it so wrong to want to be loved?*

Chapter 13: What's Wrong With Meg?

Two weeks later, the doctor finally gave his approval for Erik to make the journey into the countryside. "Remember, Mademoiselle, if you ever wish to dance for the hospital patients, the offer still stands." He made sure to tell Meg while they were waiting outside for the carriage to arrive.

"I won't forget, Monsieur. Thank you." Meg smiled.

"Now Erik, are you sure there's nothing left in your caverns that you want to take with us?" Antoinette changed the subject. Erik clutched his violin and the music box closer to him.

"I'm sure." *Everything down there is Christine...my heart...my love...* He thought bitterly.

"Very well. Here is our carriage." As Erik settled into the carriage seat, he stared out the window. It had rained not too long ago, and the city was still gray and damp, matching the feeling inside him. *So many memories...so many bitter ones... No,* he would not shed any tears. *Why should I? This home brought nothing but heartache.* And so, as they rode past the opera house, all Erik saw was a burnt-down, broken shell of what once was. And he had no desire to go back. *There is no music to be heard here.*

Bitterness numbed Erik to the effects that the two-day carriage ride would normally have on anyone else. He never looked away from the window, and yet by the time they had reached their destination, he could not recall a single landmark that they might have passed. Any tears he might have shed over the thought of leaving Christine behind were frozen inside him. What would be the point? He was tired of showing weakness in front of the Girys. *They can do nothing for me.*

Meg's uncle Robert was of course surprised to see them pulling up in front of his house, but they were made to feel welcome anyway. "You could not have come at a better time. My son Pierre has just arrived for a short visit. He will help me carry your friend inside." As if on cue, a younger gentleman appeared at the door, followed by a young lady who was introduced as Pierre's wife, Sarah. Erik felt himself growing dizzy all over again. Too many people...none of them Christine... And so, as he was carried inside, he feigned sleep. He didn't care what they thought of his face. He did not care what room they put him in. He knew it was useless to think about wanting Christine by his side, but he could not ignore that truth. He could not ignore that pain in his chest. And when he felt certain that he was alone once more, he finally allowed the tears to escape. *Oh, Christine...*

"It's about time you shed those tears." Erik's eyes snapped open. *Meg.*

"I thought I was alone." he sniffed before turning his face away from her.

"If you'd rather I leave..."

"No...wait. As long as you're here, I have one more question for you to answer." He watched her shift her gaze to the floor.

"Only one? I thought for sure I saw more in your eyes the past several days." *So you were paying attention.*

"There are more, true enough. But I only have the patience to deal with just this one."

"So ask it." Erik bit back his anger at her impatient tone. *She is no longer your prisoner.*

"In your notes, you said that it wasn't me that you feared. It could not have been Buquet, as he was dead when you told me. Who was it then?" He studied her now, watching for any unspoken response.

She let out a sigh of relief, and he raised his eyebrow. *No...best not to pursue it just yet.*

"It was my mother. I was afraid that if she knew, she'd put a stop to them." Erik laughed at that. There were very few things he feared. Antoinette's wrath was one of them. Meg looked like she might say more, but instead she kept silent. Finally, after a few moments, she spoke, but it wasn't what Erik had been expecting. "Shall I bring you some lunch?" Looking into her wide eyes, Erik once again felt something shift inside him. He suddenly longed to question her further, to unearth whatever pain she was hiding.

"Only a little, Meg. I'm not entirely hungry."

Erik set down the violin and sighed. It had been two days, but to him it felt like a lifetime of nothing but food and sleep. And music... his thoughts pointed, but the aimless tunes he played now lacked a certain...something. Oh, he knew what was missing, but to mention it even in thought would send him back into tears and longing. And then Meg would feel compelled to comfort him when he knew she would rather be elsewhere. *I did not ask her to care for me.* And yet she was there, waiting on him hand and foot as if the world itself depended on him being comfortable. He needed a break, but where could he go?

The answer presented itself the next day as Antoinette wheeled his chair into the room. Questions immediately began battling themselves for priority in his mind. *What on earth are you up to, and where on earth is Meg?* Antoinette gave him no time to ask them, however, before speaking up herself. "Meg has gone with Pierre and Sarah into town. My brother-in-law Robert thought you could use some fresh air."

"I'm comfortable here." *As long as Meg isn't coming in to bug me, I'll be fine.*

"Nonsense. Robert showed me his back garden, and I think you would enjoy it." Before Erik could protest any further, Antoinette helped him into the chair and wheeled him out the back door. As soon as his eyes adjusted to the afternoon sunlight, he had to admit that he was impressed. Rose bushes and square hedges bordered a stone pathway throughout the backyard. The winding pathway soon led past the colorful flowerbeds into the center of the yard, where a small pond sat. There was a single weeping willow on its bank, large enough to provide a peaceful, shady hiding place for anyone wishing to be alone. *Perfect.* "Where would you like to sit, Erik?" Madame Giry interrupted his thoughts, suddenly reminding him that he was still helpless and here reluctantly.

"It's all the same to me."

"Erik, you know I cannot read your mind. Just tell me what you want." *Ha. What I want?*

"It doesn't matter what I want anymore. You never asked me if I wanted to be brought to the doctor's. You never asked if I wanted to come here. Without Christine...I was ready to die. But no, you and that meddling daughter of yours pulled me back. And for what? To sit here in some stranger's garden, wishing for a life I can never have?" Erik dropped his gaze to stare at the ground and sighed. "Without Christine, I am nothing."

"Erik, it is that sort of thinking that got you into that wheelchair. If that were true, then your music, your artwork, is also nothing. Do not forget who you were before you even knew Christine existed." Antoinette walked around the wheelchair until she was in front of him. "And don't you ever let my daughter hear you talk like that. She does not deserve to bear that burden."

"She *chose* to bear it! Her notes...her interference...I didn't ask for any of it!"

"And yet she helped you anyway. Why do you think she would do that?" *Because she's foolish?* He wanted to suggest, but he knew that saying such a thing out loud would surely welcome a slap in the face. His silence triggered a sigh to escape Antoinette's lips, and she moved behind him once more. "Why don't you ponder that while sitting under that willow over there? You seem uncomfortable in this sunlight." Erik merely nodded, and he was wheeled underneath the tree's sagging branches. "I'll return with some tea. Anything else? A book perhaps?"

"Just tea will be fine." Erik's tone was a distracted one, as his mind was already replaying every single action that Meg had taken in the past few years. Her motive would be clear enough, had he only her actions to consider. Instead, her recent change of attitude left him confused, and his still-fresh feelings for Christine left him bitter and somewhat in denial. He longed to leap out of the wheelchair and dive right into the pond before him. The water looked refreshingly cold, deep enough to allow him to fully submerge himself underneath the surface. A good swim would provide ample opportunity to erase Antoinette's words...to forget about Meg and all her confusing actions.

Instead, he was forced to sit in the wheelchair, restrained by suffocating bandages. *It was that sort of thinking that got you into that wheelchair. No*, he yelled at his thoughts, *it was Raoul, and if I ever get my hands on him again, you can bet he'll regret the very day he was born!*

That evening, Erik took his meal with all the others in the dining room. As he ate, however, he grew more and more uncomfortable, sensing every eye upon him. Finally, he dropped his fork, giving up on the meal he was never hungry for in the first place. Looking up from his plate, he caught Meg watching him, but she quickly looked away. *What on earth has gotten into you?* He needed to end this. He would end her silence. Tonight.

And so, as the dishes were cleared away, Meg volunteered to guide Erik back to his room, just as he'd predicted. He held his tongue as she helped him into bed, answering in single words when she asked about his comfort. Only when she bid him good night and started for the door did he speak. "Meg?"

"What is it?" As she whirled around, Erik could see that she was biting back impatience.

"Why are you doing this? It's obvious that you'd rather be elsewhere."

"I'm sorry it seems like that, Erik, because I'm more than happy to see that you're comfortable. It's just...I don't know...I guess I've just been trying to avoid...this very thing..." Meg slid onto the bed next to him, keeping her back to him.

"Why? Wasn't it you who told me that it's bad to hold your pain inside you?"

"I'm sorry, Erik...it's something I can't discuss with you..."

"Do you not trust me? Or perhaps you don't think I would understand your pain?"

"Not this time. You'd just get angry with me." She turned to face him now, and her face was full of apology, and her eyes watered with unshed tears. "Or you'd at least laugh at me and call me 'Little Giry', as if I didn't know what I was talking about..."

"Meg, whatever it is that you have to say, I would get a lot angrier if you choose not to say it."

"I'm sorry, Erik. I really am...I would tell you if I could, believe me. It's just so complicated...I don't fully understand it myself." Standing up, she took a deep breath before turning to face him again. "I promise that I'll try harder not to distance myself from you. Can you promise to be patient with me, and wait until I'm ready to tell you?" Her eyes were wide again, pleading with him to agree with her.

"I can't promise, Meg. But I will try."

"I guess I can't expect any more than that from you, can I? Good night, Erik." Giving his hair a single stroke with her hand, she quietly let herself out of the room. In the darkness, Erik wasn't sure if he had made any progress or not. All he knew was the tingle of her hand and the echoes of her words were forefront in his mind long into the night.

Chapter 14: A Breakthrough

The next few weeks passed slowly and uneventfully, save for both Erik and Meg making the greatest effort to watch their tongues around each other. Many times, Erik found himself gritting his teeth or biting his tongue, only once or twice lashing out at the dancer. On both occasions, he cursed himself for making her cry, and then he would curse himself for caring. *My life would be a lot less complicated if she had just minded her own business.* But whatever reason she had for caring about him, he had to face the fact that she seemed to be putting him on some sort of pedestal. As if he were someone to be admired. *There's that word again.* For three years she had had shown that she admired him, and he still had no idea how he felt about it. Let alone how to act around her. *I don't deserve to be admired.*

And yet, try as he might, he could not bring himself to force her to take him off of that pedestal. *All she did was try to help. She doesn't deserve to be disappointed.* But what did she want from him? It was that single question that drove him mad every time she was near. She was always smiling around him now; her eye rolls and sighs of impatience seemed to be things of the past. Although he strongly suspected that it was all an act she was playing in his presence, he had no reason nor desire to discourage it. As long as she was speaking to him and attempting to hold conversations with each visit, he found that it helped ease the pain he was feeling, both physically and emotionally.

The topics that Meg chose to discuss were never deeper than how Erik was feeling. They usually revolved around the weather or the day's routine, subjects which Erik had little interest in. He wasn't about to tell her that, however. Avoiding discussion in regards to his pain or Christine seemed to be the best option. "Erik, are you listening?" Meg questioned out of the blue one particular afternoon. It was right after the noon meal, and the sun was still too warm to go out to the garden just yet.

"Hmm?" Erik opened his eyes, inwardly asking himself if he had really been dozing. As his mind re-adjusted to his surroundings, he tried to read the expression on Meg's face. Concern. Hurt. Confusion. She sighed for the first time (at least in his presence) in weeks.

"If you're tired, I could leave."

"I can assure you, sleep is the last thing I want right now. It seems that's all I do now." He made no effort to hide his bitterness. She had to have grown used to it, or at least expect it by now.

"Would you like your violin?"

"What's the use? My music just isn't the same without..." He stopped as soon as he saw frustration growing inside her. Sighing, he chose to rephrase the statement. "I have no inspiration nor motivation to play anything."

"What if you simply played for me?" He turned to face her then, completely puzzled. "I mean...I haven't danced in a while..." *So that's it.* What music was to him, dancing must be to her. *Of course.*

"Any particular tune in mind?" Within a half-second, his violin was in his hand, and Meg was grinning ear to ear.

"Just play anything. My dancing will take care of itself." She moved to the center of the room, and Erik placed the violin into position. *What is this hold she has on me?* He asked himself with an inward chuckle. "Anytime you're ready, Monsieur." She interrupted his thoughts, and he saw that she had crouched into a starting position. Hesitating for only a moment, he decided to start out with a soft, slow tune and see where that brought them.

As the song progressed, he watched her rise from the floor, arms out, like a flower coming into bloom. She then made a series of swirls and leaps, causing his tune to become more lively. Her dancing proved that his theory had been correct; she needed to dance. Her movements painted a picture of the freeing feeling he always got whenever he played his music, and by looking into her face, he saw that she seemed to become an entirely new person. Whatever pain she still kept inside her, he would not know it was there based on this dance alone.

He had to admire her talent. Dancing was not something he had taught himself to do; he had never seen the need for it save for the operas he composed. Even now, watching her taking countless twirls and spins, he had to wonder how she was able to keep from getting dizzy. And yet she made it seem so effortless, like breathing. He turned his attention to her footwork, immediately seeing how she'd been able to sneak around his caverns and passageways unnoticed even by him. It was then that he realized for the first time that she really could have been a help to him, had he not been so intent on pushing her away. She really was Antoinette's daughter. *Is there no room in your heart for a friend?* Her question from months before repeated itself in his mind. *Yes, I suppose there is,* he decided. He had been so set on the idea that no one would want him as a friend that he had pushed away anyone that did. But it wasn't too late. He had a second chance.

Before he realized it, Meg had stopped dancing, and Erik hurried to finish the song in a way that would satisfy them both. Meg stood then, breathless but smiling. "Thank you, Erik. I needed that."

"As did I..." Erik replied, still deep in thought. "You dance beautifully."

"And your music is absolutely wonderful, Erik. I hope you never stop composing it. The world needs to hear it." Erik's eyes widened at that remark. Christine was the only one he'd wanted to share it with.

"The question is, do they want to hear it?" Would they close their ears as soon as they see my face?

"I know I do." Meg's voice was quiet when she said this, and Erik wondered if she'd meant to say it aloud. He reached for her hand then, and as she took it, he waited until she was looking him in the eyes.

"I know you like my music, Meg, and it's very kind of you to say so. But you are kinder than most. I'm sure that there are plenty of people who don't share your opinion."

"You don't know that for sure. You need to give the world a chance."

"Me give the world a chance?" Erik scoffed. "When will the world give me a chance?"

"Mama once taught me that you shouldn't repay evil with evil...rather with good."

"I hardly think that keeping my music to myself would be considered evil, Meg." Erik raised an eyebrow.

"Yes, well, it goes for the little things too." She caressed his face then, smiling at him.

"Perhaps..." Erik's thoughts drifted with her touch, and he inwardly grasped for anything to change the subject, or at least distract her from himself. "Perhaps the sun is not as warm now." Meg glanced out the window, her face registering that he was once again correct.

"Yes...it looks to be the perfect weather for a stroll through the garden..." Her hand slipped out of his grasp as she busied herself with preparing the wheelchair.

As the summer months passed, Erik grew more and more pleasant. Perhaps it was from his change of attitude towards Meg. Perhaps it was the fresh air he was getting almost daily. Whatever it was, he felt the pain in his rib diminishing significantly as he felt this 'new' Erik taking over.

It wasn't a complete change from his old self, however. Thoughts of Christine were always forefront in his mind, even when he was playing his violin for Meg to dance to. He never let Meg know what he was thinking, however. *After all, she's still holding something back from me.* And so he vowed that until she trusted him enough to reveal her secret, he would not trust her with the deepest part of him; the empty, lonely part that kept him wide awake each night. She did not seem to suspect this; he was very good at masking his feelings by humoring her and even making some effort towards joining her in the aimless conversations that always seemed to fill the space between them.

On most afternoons when Erik requested to sit under the weeping willow, Meg would leave him alone for an hour or so while he read, played music, or just sat in deep thought. Once in a while, she would join him, whether he asked her to stay or not. They would talk, or she would lean up against the willow's trunk and doze. Strangely enough, even when she was there without him asking, he never felt as though he were being intruded upon. In the months since the opera house fire, Meg had somehow become a constant in his life. He hadn't asked for it. He had even fought against it. But, just as her mother before her, she proved that she could withstand anything he threw at her. In his weakness, pain, and helplessness, he had learned to tolerate her presence and her caring touch. He wondered about the future; when his rib healed, would Meg still be there? An old part of himself reminded him that he really shouldn't care either way. Something had changed, regardless, and a good part of himself hated it. *It's Christine I want...I still need her. I love her.*

It was this train of thought that put him in a sour mood one afternoon, when the gray clouds overhead matched what he was feeling. The smell of rain was in the air, but he didn't care. "I'll sit under the willow today."

"Are you sure?" Meg looked up at the sky.

"Of course I'm sure." His tone was harsh, but his mind was too busy for him to think about apologizing. Silently, Meg pushed the wheelchair through the grass and past the sagging branches of the willow. She had brought along a book of poetry, but Erik didn't feel like reading. Scowling at the pond before him, he only vaguely noticed her settle onto the ground, her attention soon focused on the descriptive pages. *Good. It will be silent.* Oh, if only that were true, for not ten minutes later, the air was filled with the sound of a sudden downpour. Not missing a beat, he heard Meg squeal behind him as the book was dropped, and in a blur of light blue fabric, the dancer was soon across the pond from him, twirling and laughing in the rain. Her arms spread out beside her, her eyes closed, she tilted her head back, as if to taunt the falling droplets. *You may dampen the ground, but you cannot dampen my spirit!* She seemed to be saying. The corners of Erik's mouth twitched ever so slightly, and before he knew it, he was laughing along with her. As he laughed, he felt something break free inside him. Soon, tears of laughter turned into tears he had kept hidden away for so long; unshed tears for the love he had lost. *Why now?* It was so sudden, and yet he couldn't stop the flood of tears. It was as if he was saying good bye to Christine all over again. Keeping his eyes on Meg, he finally realized what had triggered it. *Why can't I be laughing with Christine? Sharing her delight in the simple things...*

But what had brought delight to Christine, other than music? Had he even thought to ask her? He thought back to all the times he had witnessed her smile. She loved flowers, he had learned that right off. She loved spending time with Meg and the other girls living in the opera house dormitories. He also knew without a doubt that she loved being onstage; the night of her debut made that idea all the clearer. And while he was thinking about that night, he remembered how her face had lit up when Raoul had entered the room. The two hadn't seen each other in years, and yet her joy at the sight of him went back much further than he had known her. Clenching his fists, his tears flowed even more at the thought.

"Marguerite Elizabeth Giry, get back inside this instant! Are you trying to catch your death of cold?" Antoinette's shrill voice rang out, interrupting his thoughts. "Erik, are you all right?" She approached him from the side as Meg paused mid-twirl, completely surprised at her mother's sudden appearance. Erik quickly brushed at the tears, but they kept falling as Meg joined them under the branches.

"I'm sorry, Mama...Erik...I did not mean to leave you alone so suddenly..."

"Never mind apologizing. Just get inside and change out of those wet clothes." Antoinette placed the poetry book into her daughter's hands, and Meg was quick to obey. Holding an umbrella over Erik's head, Madame Giry wheeled him through the garden and into the shelter of the house. She remained silent as she helped him into his bed. Handing him a cup of tea, she finally spoke. "I have sent word to the doctor. He should be coming within the next few days to check on your injury." By now, Erik's tears had slowed, and Antoinette brushed away the few remaining on his face. "Erik, I wish there was something I could say to take away your heartache."

"Then don't try. Just leave me." Erik sniffled, turning his head away. As soon as he heard the door close, he set the untouched cup of tea on the bedside table and watched the rain continue to fall outside the window. *I wish you were here... I know we must say good bye...*

Chapter 15: Meg's Birthday

The doctor arrived as scheduled. Upon close examination, he finally decided that Erik could start trying to walk again. "Take plenty of caution, Monsieur. Do not try to rush it," he warned while removing the bandages. Erik muttered a quick thank you, relieved to be free of the suffocating bandages. "I suggest you stay in bed today. Tomorrow, you may try to get up, but be sure someone is there to help you. Do not twist your torso around any more than you have to." As the list of instructions went on, Erik couldn't help rolling his eyes. Finally, the doctor headed for the door, then stopped and turned. *Now what?* "I'm going to suggest that a bath be drawn for you. A good long soak in hot water should help to relax your muscles." Erik nodded, not trusting himself to speak as he grew more and more impatient. Seeming to take the subtle hint, the doctor exited the room. Not one to take orders from anyone, Erik slowly raised himself on his elbows. Feeling no immediate pain, he swung his legs over the side of the bed. Still nothing. Hesitating only long enough to make sure the door was still closed, he placed all his weight on his feet and stood. He never got a chance to take a single step, however. Grimacing at the pain, he collapsed back onto the mattress. *Curses.* Just then, the door opened, and within seconds, Meg was at his side.

"Oh, Erik, can't you listen to the doctor for once?" Grasping his legs, she rotated him so that he was fully on the bed once more.

"For your information, I am fine. I collapsed only from being off my feet for so long."

"You're lying." She was staring him in the eyes now, and he met her gaze stubbornly. "Now, Erik, I will be leaving tomorrow for Paris. Can you promise that I won't come back to find you even more injured?"

"You're leaving?" Erik raised an eyebrow at her, his mind racing.

"Yes...Mama and I will be gone for a week. I will be visiting the hospital to dance for the patients, and Mama wants to see if any progress has been made at the opera house." Seeming to notice the alarm in his face, Meg brushed her hand through his hair. "It's only a week, Erik. We will be back, and I expect you to be in full health. Can you promise me that you'll not rush it?"

"Just worry about your dancing, Meg. Go. Enjoy yourself." Erik threw her a half-smile, and it seemed to suffice. Returning the smile, she turned and left him alone. He had dreaded this. He wasn't ready to face his thoughts and opinions towards the little dancer. But now she was leaving, and he would be left alone in a house full of strangers. At that thought, panic rose up inside him. In all the time he'd been here, he had only seen glimpses of Robert, Pierre, and Sarah; glimpses upon which he had no basis as to whether or not he could trust them. For the first time in months, he longed for his mask, suddenly feeling very insecure. All that was familiar to him was now slipping through his fingers, and he could do nothing about it. *Curses!* At least with the bandages, he'd felt he had a reason to feel helpless. *Surely I will go mad before this week is over.*

That evening, it was Madame Giry who came to check on Erik before they all turned in for the night. "Erik, I have a small favor to ask of you."

"What can I possibly do for you when I apparently can't even leave this bed?"

"It's not for me...as it turns out, we will be returning the day before Meg's eighteenth birthday. I was wondering if...perhaps while you are here, you might do something for her."

"Such as...?"

"I don't know. Use that genius, creative mind of yours and come up with something. She thinks so highly of you, Erik, and I have never been able to give her much..."

"Say no more. I'll see what I can do." Erik sighed.

"Thank you, Erik. And not a word to Meg about this...I want her to be completely surprised."

"Madame Giry, surprises are my specialty." Erik smirked, and Antoinette laughed.

"Yes, of course they are! Well, good night, Erik. We will see you in the morning to bid you good bye."

"Sleep well, Antoinette." Erik squeezed her hand reassuringly, and Antoinette nodded before heading upstairs.

By the end of the week, all Erik knew for sure was that he'd survived. The first night of Meg's absence, he had slipped into a nightmare-filled sleep, after which he could only sob into his pillow. Sometimes he called for Christine, other times he cried out for Meg, and that frightened him even more. After singing a bit to himself, he was finally able to get his tears under control, but he could not say that he'd allowed himself to sleep any more the rest of the week.

Aside from assisting him in his attempts to walk, Antoinette's in-laws generally left Erik alone. He used this time to work on his gift to Meg. He had never celebrated his own birthday, having no knowledge as to what day it actually fell on. But Meg deserved something in return for all her help; she deserved to know that her friendship was appreciated. Not having the materials to create what she really deserved, his gift was a simple sketch on plain paper with charcoal. Certainly nothing compared to the endless creations he had made for Christine, but it would have to do. He only hoped that she wouldn't be disappointed.

Erik only vaguely remembered hearing the commotion at the door. They must have gotten a late start that morning, he decided, for it was well after sunset when they arrived. He was thankful that they were considerate enough to go right up to bed; he was exhausted from both waiting for them and making extra effort in his attempts to walk on his own.

The next morning, he positioned himself in the hallway at the foot of the stairs, seated in the wheelchair. Meg would appear any moment now, and he couldn't wait to see her reaction. Just when he was about to climb the stairs himself, she was there, wearing a blueish-green dress full of ruffles and lace. Her hair was in two thin braids tied back, forming a sort of crown or halo in the morning sun peaking through the window. Her eyes lit up when she saw him, but the smile faded when she saw that he was still in his wheelchair. "Oh, Erik, please don't tell me that you injured yourself further." She paused three steps up from him, and he couldn't hold back any longer. Twisting his face into a cringe of mock-pain, he raised himself from the chair and extended his hand. As she took it, he placed his lips on the back of her fingers.

"Happy birthday, Meg." He smiled and kept her hand in his grip as she descended the last of the stairs.

"Erik, are you sure you're all right?" Meg studied his face.

"Of course I'm sure. Now then, might I escort you to the breakfast table?" She merely nodded, completely in awe at the change in his manner. Her shock did not stop her from taking his elbow, and they made their way to the dining room in silence.

After breakfast, Erik asked if Meg would join him in the garden for a stroll. He made a quick stop at his room to retrieve the bound parcel, and Meg eyed it curiously until they were out among the flower beds. "I'm afraid it's not much..." Suddenly nervous and unsure about proper proceedings for this occasion, he could not find anymore words to say. He was grateful when she took the gift from him and eagerly unwrapped the brown paper to reveal the sketch. He waited for a smile...for a thank you...but none came. Instead, she burst into tears, shoving the sketch back at him before racing back inside. Completely puzzled and hurt, Erik studied the paper in his hand. It was Meg in a dancing position, her arms raised while her feet looked as though she were about to go into a spin. Her hair was tied back in a loose bun, and her face...*Curses!* Her face was Christine's.

Before he could consider his next actions, the door swung open and Antoinette appeared, her eyes filled with rage. *Oh, here it comes.* Bracing himself, he didn't dare to speak. "Erik, I want an answer from you! What on earth were you thinking? How could you dare to hurt her like this, on her birthday no less, when she has done nothing but care about you?" She grabbed the sketch from him, but instead of looking at it, she shoved it pointedly in his face.

"I'm so sorry...I...I don't know how that happened..."

"Oh really? Because it is very clear to me! You cannot let go of her! You cannot face facts! And if you keep this up, you won't even have me or my daughter to help you. You'll die a bitter, lonely man. Is that what you want?"

"No...I..."

"You are to go inside and apologize to my daughter. And then you are going to find some way to make this up to her. And I don't care how you do it, but you will figure out how you are going to deal with the fact that Christine is a married woman now, and you need to move on." With that, Antoinette turned on her heel and marched inside. Erik soon followed, tearing up the drawing as he went.

It was easy to predict where Meg might have gone. Climbing the stairs, the sound of her sobs met his ears. He found her door, gingerly knocking. "Meg?"

"Oh, go away! I'll be fine!" Her words were betrayed by a loud sniffle, and Erik quietly opened the door and peaked in. Meg was sprawled across her bed, face buried in a pillow. "I said go away! Don't you ever listen to me?"

"Do you mind if I sit? That was the first time I've climbed stairs ever since the injury..."

"Do what you like. I don't care." She sat up, but kept her back to him as he slid onto the mattress. Slowly, he reached out and touched her shoulder. She flinched, but did not pull away.

"Meg, that is furthest from the truth. You've done nothing but care for the past three years."

"And where has that gotten me?" She finally turned to face him, and he studied her red, puffy eyes before replying.

"Meg, you've got to believe me when I say that that drawing was a mistake. My mind slipped...I wasn't thinking."

"Forget the drawing! She's always going to be your main focus, isn't she? She's always going to have the biggest part of your heart. You're always going to love her more!"

"Meg, is that why you didn't want to return for her wedding? You're jealous of her?"

"I don't want to be...it's not like I hate her or anything...I just...oh, it doesn't matter what I think. You said yourself I will never earn your pity, so why should I expect you to love me?" With every word that passed through her lips, Erik felt his head spin. Seeming to see his bewilderment, Meg let out a scoff. "Yes, Erik, I love you, all right? And it's not like I planned on it or anything, but it happened anyway. That's what I couldn't tell you before. Because I was still confused...and because it would be useless to tell you when I know you'll never love me back!"

"Oh, Meg..." Erik clutched his chest as tears welled up in his eyes. *She* loves *me?* She *loves* me?

All of a sudden, he couldn't breathe, and he began pacing the floor. "But nobody loves me!"

"You've never given them the chance to! You've always been so focused on Christine that you've pushed everyone else away!"

"I know that, Meg. I know that now." He approached the bed once more and sat down next to her, gathering her in his arms. "I am so sorry, Meg. I should have seen it..." His words faded as his thoughts took over, and he was only vaguely aware of the constant feeling of her head on his shoulder. Suddenly, everything was making sense. The letters, her distance, her caring touch...it was all so obvious, and he inwardly kicked himself for not seeing it before now. He was still unsure of how he felt toward her. He needed time to think. "Meg, I promise I'll make it up to you. Will you forgive me? Give me time to think things over?"

"I suppose that's fair." Meg sniffled before lifting her head.

"And Meg, you really are a beautiful dancer and a lovely young woman." Erik gave her a weak smile, gently tracing her jawline while using his thumb to dry her tears. Slowly, she returned the smile and looked away. "Happy birthday, Meg. The world should count itself lucky that you were born."

"Thank you, Erik." He thought he saw her blush, but he said no more and left the room.

Chapter 16: Facing the Future

Erik spent the rest of the day in the garden, only coming in for the birthday celebration at suppertime. Meg had changed into a pale purple dress, and there was not a trace of her earlier tears on her face. Instead, she showed nothing but pure delight as the events passed and as the gifts were given. Antoinette would occasionally steal a questioning glance at Erik, but he kept his face straight. He was still confused, and he didn't dare show any emotion just yet.

Just when Meg was setting aside what appeared to be the final gift, Erik stood. "Wait here, Meg." He ignored all the confused faces and hurried to his room. Grasping the item he'd come for, he quickly made his way back to the sitting room and presented the gift to the birthday girl. His gesture was met with gasps from both Meg and Antoinette.

"Erik, are you sure?" Meg questioned.

"I hope it brings as much joy to you as it has to me." Placing the monkey music box in her lap, he returned to his seat across the room.

"Thank you, Erik. I know how much this means to you... I'll cherish it forever." Erik merely nodded at this statement, not trusting himself to speak. He could not ignore the shift inside him as he watched the smile spread across her face as she wound up the music box. *She really is quite beautiful.*

That night, Erik tossed and turned for hours, but not for the same reasons he'd always had. Instead of being tortured by thoughts of Christine, his mind was filled with thoughts and images of Meg over the years he'd known her. There were very few real memories he had of her; curious and stubborn as she was, she had always shrunk into the shadows of her mother and of Christine. With that in mind, it was quite easy to see how he had been able to overlook her. *Not to mention that she is Antoinette's daughter...no telling what Antoinette would have done to me had I even thought of seeking Meg out!*

Christine's arrival had erased that possibility anyway. A new thought dawned on him just then. In her vulnerable state, it was easy for Christine to be fooled by Erik's tricks and lies. She was ready to believe anything...anything that might give her comfort over the death of her father. But Meg was different. She had seen right through his deception even from the start. She would not be fooled that easily, being Antoinette's daughter. She saw past his smoke and mirrors, past his mask and alter-ego. *And she still loves me.* She had seen his biggest strengths and yet stood by him in his weakest moments. She had kept his feelings in mind every time she spoke, not out of fear, but out of consideration. She had even been ready to forget her own desires while he still pined after Christine. *Oh, Meg...*

As the weeks passed and as Erik grew more accustomed to walking around on his own, there were many moments when he would catch himself missing Meg's caring touch and helping hand. She was distancing herself again, but it was different now. She was giving him the space he needed, and he appreciated her consideration. Yet whenever she was away from him, there was a constant pang of longing inside him, and he couldn't help but wonder if he would always feel this way if she were to ever leave again.

Autumn was now upon them, and with it came a chill that kept Erik inside most days. When he did venture outside, he would walk around the edge of the yard, deep in thought. He could usually feel Meg's eyes upon him from the glass doors, but he never glanced her way. He didn't dare to, for fear that if he did...*no...she has to understand...I'm just not ready...*

These days, he wasn't sure what he was feeling. Perhaps it was sadness, perhaps uncertainty towards the future. His head still spun with confusion, and he sometimes wondered if he told Meg that he returned her feelings, would it be like he was settling? Meg did not deserve that. She may have chosen to stay in Christine's shadow all those years, but this was certainly different. She deserved to be loved by someone who would always put her first. And he wasn't exactly sure that he was ready to do that. After all, Christine...

And then he realized that Christine didn't mean as much to him anymore. Christine had chosen Raoul long ago. She had not stayed by Erik's side through his fever and his injury. To be sure, she had brought a single spark into his life that showed him what it felt like to love someone. Meg, on the other hand, was a burning torch that had lit up his caverns, even when he had treated her like a prisoner. And if she were to leave...he suddenly couldn't bear that thought. *I need her in my life.*

"You're not planning on running, are you?" Erik jumped and whirled around. He had been staring into the patch of woods surrounding the yard, so lost in thought that he hadn't heard her footsteps through the drying grass and fallen leaves. Composing himself, he allowed a reassuring smile to spread across his face.

"Don't worry, Little Giry. I remember what happened last time...I'm not a fool to try that again."

"You miss her though, don't you?" They stared at each other then, trying to see past the mask of formalities and careful politeness. With a sigh, Erik slowly nodded his head and glanced down at the ground beside her feet.

"Yes, I miss her, Meg. Not so much that I'd risk my life or your happiness, but...I miss her." In the silence that followed, he noticed her shiver ever so slightly. He immediately took off his coat and wrapped it around her shoulders. She responded by glancing up at him, a sad but grateful smile on her face. "You miss her too. I can see it in your face." Her burst into tears confirmed this statement, and he turned her around and pulled her into an embrace. After a few moments of feeling her face buried against his chest and her shoulders shaking beneath his arms, he suddenly felt the need to erase every single tear from her eyes and stand between her and anything that might bring her pain. After all, hadn't she wiped at his tears so many times before? *Don't be selfish, Erik. Don't be a fool. Christine is gone...Meg is here now, but she won't be for long. Don't wait until it's too late...* Inwardly nodding in response to his thoughts, he gently placed his hand under her chin, lifting her head so he could study her tear-streaked face. *She's beautiful...precious...* Slowly, he lowered his face to her level, and before he knew what was happening, his lips were touching hers.

At first, he was unsure, ready to pull away and apologize for being forward. Then he felt her lips respond, parting ever so slightly to allow the love to pass between them. He held her closer, his fingers running through the back of her golden hair. He felt her arms wrap around his neck, and suddenly, tears of his own were starting to fall. Finally, they pulled away, but Erik kept his hands on her shoulders as he let the tears take over. "You love me." He knew that for sure now. Unlike his first kiss, he knew that this was not one out of pity. It was love...real love...and the feeling was overwhelming him.

"Yes, Erik. I really do love you." Meg reached up and brushed at his tears. He then realized that his coat had fallen to the ground, and he picked it back up, brushing off the leaves before placing it back on her shoulders. They embraced again, letting the tears run their course before either one dared to speak. At first, Erik couldn't identify the reason behind their tears. But as he felt her sigh mere seconds after he had let out a sigh of his own, he realized that what they were feeling was total relief. Relief that they were loved in return. Relief that there were no more secrets between them. Nothing left to hide behind. He had never reached this with anyone, and all it took was a quiet little dancing girl to bring him to this place. Uncertainty aside, he was no longer frightened about the future. Whatever he was meant to face, Meg would be there beside him.

Except...there was still one last thing hanging over his head. With a deep breath, he began to sing about facing one's past. Looking down at Meg's puzzled expression, he let a weak smile spread across his face. "After all, our future lies before us now. We cannot afford to look back with regrets any longer." Taking a moment to bury his nervousness and doubts, he went on. "Meg, before we can do that, I think we both owe Christine a visit and an apology."

"Erik, you can't! Raoul will..."

"I know what Raoul said, and if he wishes to have the entire police force present, he may. But I need to do this. I need to apologize to them both and say good bye." *I need to be sure...* "And, Meg, she is your best friend. You can't let me come between you."

"Oh, Erik...I know you're right...just please be careful." She leaned back into him then, and he responded with another kiss to the top of her head.

A month later, Erik stood in front of the opera house doors, Meg's hand locked in his nervous grip. The street was quiet. But then, with no opera, there would not be the usual crowds. It was mid-morning anyway, and in the middle of the week.

They had reached the doctor's house the previous evening. The doctor in question had been more than pleased to see Erik's progress, and he once again asked Meg if she would dance for the hospital patients. "Perhaps in a couple days." Meg had replied with a tired smile. Erik and Antoinette had exchanged a quick glance then. If things went as planned, this would perhaps be one of Meg's last opportunities to perform. She had never reached the title of Prima Ballerina, the dream of every girl that came through the opera house doors. *Yes, Doctor, Meg will dance. Even if I have to play for her.* It was a silent promise, but no less important.

But first, they had today to get through. Erik squeezed Meg's hand even tighter. "This is going to hurt isn't it?" It was not a question that required an answer, and she did not provide any. Erik already knew the answer, and he clutched his chest ever so slightly.

"Shall we go in then?" Antoinette broke the silence from behind them, climbing the steps and pausing in front of the door to look back at them. She raised an eyebrow, and Erik nodded.

He did not remember walking. All he remembered was passing through the doors to face the grand hall, where he had made his first appearance at the Masquerade Ball. No longer was it filled with extravagant decor; instead, dust had built up on the gold-painted railing. Further in, and he was passing the rows and rows of floor seats, and he was surprised that any had survived at all. He couldn't help but scowl at them; only in his dreams had he been allowed to place himself within the multitude of opera-goers. Which was why he had requested Box Five. But no...that was all in the past. *Time to move on.*

As they reached the remains of the massive chandelier, he felt Meg stiffen beside him. *Why would Raoul pick this place?* He could only imagine the frightening memories that were passing through his companions' minds at this moment. He did not have to think about his own memories of that night. Or rather, he did not dare to. He let go of Meg's hand; instead opting to wrap his arm around her shoulders and pull her close. Turning to her, he whispered ever so softly, "Help me..."

He had just enough time to plant a kiss on her forehead before Raoul broke the tense silence. "My word, Christine. He actually showed." Erik slowly turned around, taking every precious second to stamp out the urge to resort to his old methods. "Before you say your peace, Monsieur(*or was it 'Monster'?* Erik couldn't tell), allow me to take some precautionary measures. Officers!" At that single word, Erik heard footsteps behind him, apparently approaching from the orchestra pit. Before he could "congratulate" the

Vicompte for his strategy, Erik felt his arms yanked behind his back, thick ropes binding his wrists together. He grit his teeth against the pain and humiliation, locking his eyes on the younger man now sneering at him.

"Monsieur, is all this really necessary?" Antoinette's voice was strained with the effort to keep calm.

"Madame Giry, I warned you. It is your fault for not taking me seriously. Nevertheless, I must protect my wife." As he spoke those last two words, Raoul's gaze darted back in Erik's direction, daring him to argue the fact.

"Protect her from what? Erik has done nothing to deserve this, and I can assure you that he does not plan on it either! He's changed! If only you would listen!" Meg had apparently recovered from her shock, and she was using every ounce of her logic and reason now.

"Mademoiselle, this is no place for you. Perhaps you and Christine could go somewhere to talk in private. I'm sure you have plenty of catching up to do. Madame Giry...?" He threw a hinting glance at the ballet instructor, who reluctantly nodded.

"Come along, ladies."

"But Mama..." Meg protested.

"Don't worry, my dear. Erik will be all right." Her words were directed at Meg, but there was no mistaking her glare at the Vicompte. It was not a false encouragement. It was a promise, and she was daring the young man to contradict her.

The women had no sooner left the room when Raoul's hand came flying at Erik's throat, forcing the former Phantom to look him in the eyes. "Look around you! Look! See what your selfishness and greed has done! Your money will not cover this. It was not even your money to give!" Raoul removed his hand then, wiping it on his trousers before unsheathing his sword. Touching the point to Erik's chest, he continued. "This was never your theater. It was never your home in which you could order us around. No. It was your little hideaway. A hideaway for the criminal you are! You are a murderer three times over, and that's not counting the innocent souls lost in the fire. No, your home is behind bars for the rest of your long, miserable life. You see, I won't kill you. But I will make you pay." At that, Erik felt the many hands that had been holding him drop. Before he could think of his next move, however, his nose cracked under Raoul's fist, and he dropped to the floor. *Not again...* But there were no more punches. Instead, Raoul stood over him, sword aimed at his throat. Erik stared up at him, then glanced around at the crowd of police assembled. All of a sudden, he was back at the fair, and old tears were threatening to pour down to meet the blood on his face. *No...I won't give up. Not yet. This is not over.* "Perhaps you would care for a taste of your own medicine. The water trap, perhaps? A nice swim before you are transferred to your new permanent residence?"

"Raoul, wait!" Christine cried out, and she soon appeared with Meg and Antoinette not far behind. The narrow blade was removed from his skin, but remained in Erik's eyesight. He wasn't looking at the sword, however.

"Christine, you shouldn't be here..." Raoul's voice reflected his torn emotions as he weighed his priorities.

"Let him speak." Before Raoul could respond to his wife's pleading words, Meg knelt behind Erik's head, raising him so she could place her lap underneath him as a pillow. Now facing the newlyweds, Erik felt himself growing dizzy from the loss of blood. *Not yet!* He scolded his body.

"P--please...forgive me...I...want to live...give me the chance to try..." The words were sung in a hoarse, weak voice, not his best performance, but the meaning was there as he faded into unconsciousness.

He had said what he had come to say, and that was what mattered.

Chapter 17: Surviving

When he awoke, he was still in the same position. Only a few minutes had passed, but the ropes had been removed. "Meg loves him, Raoul. She told me while we were in the other room. The fear is gone...it's over." Christine was saying. The doctor appeared then, blocking Erik's view of Raoul's reaction. He was then helped to his feet and moved to one of the remaining seats toward the back of the theater.

"Now lean forward, Monsieur, to keep from swallowing any blood." The doctor instructed, handing him a handkerchief. Closing his eyes from the dizziness, he was only vaguely aware of the doctor leaving his side, and Meg sliding into the seat next to him. They were silent for the longest time, until Erik started shaking with sobs.

"Erik?" Meg placed her hand on his shoulder.

"How could I have been so foolish? I walked right into his trap..." Erik shifted the handkerchief before continuing. "I should have just sent her a note and been done with it."

"Erik, you couldn't have known! Please don't put yourself down. I know how much Christine means to you, and you to her. It's only right that you wanted to patch things up with her."

"But look where it got me! I was back in the fair all over again...helpless...being beaten in front of a crowd...and now you have to see me like this..."

"Oh Erik..." She reached over and traced the right side of his face. "Yes it pains me to see you hurting now. But I love you, and I want to be by your side no matter what. You don't have to feel ashamed in front of me." She pulled him close to her, and they were silent once more, waiting for the blood and tears to dry.

After several minutes, the doctor reappeared. "Whenever you're ready, Monsieur, I can take care of your nose back at my house." Erik wiped at his tears one more time before responding.

"Yes...yes I'm ready now..." He ignored the dizziness as he stood, but graciously accepted Meg's supporting arm as they followed the doctor out of the opera house. A steady rain was now falling, and Erik had no doubt that it would turn to snow or at least frozen rain any moment. He pulled Meg even closer then, protecting her from the late autumn chill.

The walk was a short one, and Erik was soon seated inside the doctor's office. While Meg cleaned the dried blood off his face, the doctor prepared the bandages that would eventually cover his broken nose. For how long, he wasn't sure, but at least he wouldn't be confined to beds and wheelchairs again. For that, he was grateful, and yet he didn't feel that it made up for Raoul causing that helpless feeling to build up inside him in front of everyone he cared about. And yet...

Could he really fault Raoul for protecting Christine from the unknown? She was fragile, after all, and he had every right to protect his wife. After all, Erik did not have the best reputation. Raoul couldn't have known about the changes that had taken place inside him. *Besides...*Erik thought with a sigh...*if we keep attacking each other, neither of us will find true peace with ourselves and with each other. We both need to move on.*

A knock at the door pulled him from his thoughts then, and Antoinette entered. "Erik, Meg, you have visitors." Meg looked up at Erik, questions in her eyes. Erik nodded at her before speaking.

"Let them in." Antoinette stepped aside, and the Vicompte and Vicomptess came into the small room. There was a look of caution on both their faces, and Erik surprised himself with his calm, cheerful manner. "Christine? Raoul?"

"Hello, Erik...it is Erik, right?" Christine allowed a careful smile to spread across her face. "I...I just want to say that I'm sorry..."

"Christine, you have nothing to apologize for. I only ask for your forgiveness."

"But I am sorry...I betrayed you..."

"Oh yes...that..." Erik paused as the memory of the public unmasking flashed through his mind. "I can forgive you for that, Christine, as I never should have deceived you in the first place. Please, speak no more of that night."

"Before we bury that memory completely, Erik..." Raoul spoke up, "perhaps we can make some sort of deal..." Erik raised an eyebrow at this suggestion.

"And what deal might that be?" His tone was not cold; instead it was full of caution. He would not be made a fool again.

"It seems we are in need of someone to oversee the reconstruction of the opera house. If you take the job, I will see that the charges against you are dropped. You will not be paid, mind you, and you must see that all your traps and secret doors are sealed up for good."

"What about his caves?" Meg questioned, and Erik nearly jumped, having almost forgotten her presence in the room. Meg continued speaking, apparently unaware of the expression on his face. "His artwork and possessions...what happens to them?"

"Those items that he built or created himself, he may keep. If there is anything down there that were taken from the opera house, Erik, it must be returned."

"Fair enough..." Erik was deep in thought now, unsure as to whether or not he was ready to face that part of his past just yet. He remembered how painful it had been last time, and he knew that this would be a true test of his willingness to move on. As if sensing his hesitation, Meg took a hold of his hand and gave it a reassuring squeeze. Erik squeezed back, thanking her with a smile. "I accept."

The reconstruction began almost immediately, funded by Raoul and by the enormous salary Erik had accumulated. As the opera house took shape once more, it came to their attention that Monsieurs Andre and Firmin had wiped their hands of the theater business once and for all. Not wanting to leave the opera house empty for any longer than was necessary, Erik sold many of his art pieces, songs, and operas. With the money he earned, he was able to purchase the Opera Populaire and become manager. Thankfully, Carlotta had decided to retire by then, and Erik was grateful for that one less headache he would have to endure.

Meg did end up performing many times for the hospital patients, with Erik accompanying her with his violin. Just as he'd thought, she never did make it to Prima Ballerina, but she would eventually become the next ballet mistress when Antoinette felt that she herself could no longer perform those duties. In the meantime, Erik and Meg did marry a year after the re-opening, and together they raised five children, whose talents proved to be a major contribution to the opera house.

On many occasions, Erik would find letters tucked away in the most interesting places, places that only Meg, the mystery writer would know or think about. She always made herself scarce when he read them, but would always enter the room minutes later with a secretive smile on her face. Erik would then raise an eyebrow, but he never mentioned the contents of the letters. "How is little Alyce doing with her routine?" he would ask of their youngest daughter.

"She is showing great potential, Erik, as usual. And how is the next opera coming along?"

"Fine, fine," Erik would reply with a grin, and their day would go on as normal.

On one afternoon, in their later years, Erik was hunched over the organ, muttering under his breath at the notes that refused to work together. It was then he noticed a corner of white paper sticking up ever so slightly from between two of the keys. *No wonder the notes are off. Mess around with my instruments, hmm, Meg? You'll pay for that later...* Smirking to himself, he unfolded the paper. It was not one of her more personal, playful letters, however, and he read it twice.

"Dearest Erik,

Forgive me for the seriousness of this letter, dearest husband, but I've been thinking lately of all we have been through. And I've come to wonder...do you regret any of it?

Always yours,

Meg"

Once he had overcome his initial puzzlement over the tone of the note, he pondered only a few moments before starting a note of his own.

"Dearest Meg,

Where on earth did that come from? But then the day I fully understand that mind of yours is the day I allow Carlotta back into the limelight. Ha!

To answer your question, my dear, no, I do not regret any of it. I take that back. I do regret the way I treated you right after I found out who you were. You didn't deserve any of that. But otherwise, Meg, everything we have gone through has served to bring us closer together. Many of my early memories are painful to recall, but without them, I would have never learned to appreciate the healing light you have brought to my very soul. I still have yet to figure out how I could have ever deserved you. But I suppose that is a mystery for the ages. I can only hope that I have given you everything you desire. You deserve the world and more for loving me, Meg. Don't ever settle for anything less than just that.

Your loving husband,

Erik"

"Oh, Erik..." Meg wrapped her arms around his neck as soon as she'd read the letter. He was sitting in his armchair, and she had placed herself on the arm of it. Smiling, he pulled her onto his lap and held her close to him, feeling her tears of joy against his skin. "Erik, you exaggerate."

"Oh, but it's all true, Meg. I meant every word of it." His lips swept across her face, kissing away the tears that had escaped, until they came to a stop on her own lips. "Now then, my little dancer, about you playing around with my instrument..."

Moments later, a squeal of delight pierced the silence of the night.

Story Two: Regarding Joseph Buquet

A/N: This short story comes from my fan fiction imagination mind wanting to find a reason for everything Erik did. I refuse to let my readers think that he 'kills without a thought' as Christine believed. True enough I did rationalize this incident in my earlier story, "Phantom Letters', but that reasoning relied on Erik receiving a mystery letter about Joseph Buquet. This time, his reasoning started way back, to his childhood. As always, I do not own 'Phantom of the Opera' or any of its characters.

Dearest Antoinette,

I realize I must have caused much shock and pain and confusion tonight with the murder of Joseph Buquet. For that, I hope you can accept my deepest apology. However, please understand that Joseph Buquet had it coming to him, and I would have done it over and over again. Forgive me. I know that makes me sound heartless, but he is one of the very few who I strongly believe deserved to die by my hand. Now, please, dear friend, I beg of you to hear me out on this matter. You have stood by and watched me do many things, and you have not tried to interfere. For that I owe you much, including this explanation.

I knew Joseph Buquet. I knew him longer than I knew you. He was the son of the man you saw me kill at the fair. He had no talents...no gifts...nothing that would cause his father to put him on display. He was supposed to have helped run the different shows from behind the scenes, as he did here. But he was lazy, always getting into trouble. Many of my beatings were caused by lies he made up to hide his own crimes and pranks. As if that was not enough, his laughter and taunting made up about half of all the voices I am haunted with each night.

How he came to be at the opera house, I did not know until I caught up with him a week ago, in the alleyway behind the opera house. This is the conversation which followed, as best as I can remember it.

"Joseph Buquet." I called out to the drunken man who had stumbled over to a crate, tripping into a sitting position. He lowered the bottle from his lips, squinting his eyes in order for him to see who was talking.

"Do I know you?" His question was followed by a belch, yet I managed to ignore that enough in order to step closer.

"It is I who know you, Buquet, as I suspect that you think I died, or was arrested, long before now. No, you do not know me. You know me as the Opera Ghost. The Phantom of the Opera. Or, even further back, the....Devil's Child?" By now I was bending over his pathetic body, and I smirked as his face reflected recognition.

"No...It can't be!"

"Can't it?" I smirked even more, mostly to hide my nervousness about what I was about to do. Before I could have second thoughts, I slid the mask off of my face, forcing myself to meet his eyes. Oh, he was surprised at first. But then the corners of his mouth turned up into an all-too-familiar smile, and I replaced the mask.

"So it is you. I take it you grew out of that potato sack."

"Why did you come here?"

"Needed fresh air." He shrugged.

"I mean, why did you come to the opera house? What happened to your father's fair?"

"Oh don't think you don't know! You killed him! I saw you...you killed my father and then ran off like the coward you have always been!"

"Coward? You call me a coward when it was I who took the brunt of your beatings for you?"

"Ah, he would have beaten you anyway. Why should both our backsides hurt?" Another shrug. Another sip from his bottle. That is, before I knocked it out of his hand. He wiped his hand across his beard angrily, standing up. Or at least trying to. "I wasn't finished that. You owe me a drink."

"I owe you far more than that, Joseph Buquet. Do not think I have not seen you stealing glances at the chorus girls and dancers when you should be doing your job. And then you grab the first one you can find, whether she wants your filthy hands on her or not, pretending you're the least bit desirable."

"Look who's talking about desirable all of a sudden!" He laughed, but for once I was unphased.

"At least I know that I'm not. At least I know my place. Perhaps you should learn yours!" I shoved him back down to his seat, although it did not take much strength on my part to do so. "Now. Answer my question. How did you come to work here instead of the fair?"

"Never did like the fair anyway. I was only there because of my father. Even then I would have run off long before he died, but I suppose I was having too much fun with you." He was smirking again, but I said nothing. "After you murdered my father and escaped, I sold the fair to the fortune teller and left. Did odd jobs over the years just to get by. Then I saw this place was looking for stagehands. End of story."

"And you became a drunk in the process, I see."

"Took away the pain and anger I was feeling." Shrug. I sighed and walked a few feet away before turning around.

"Very well. If you do your job...and only your job, to the best of your ability, I will leave you in peace. But touch one more chorus girl or dancer...touch one more drop of liquor when you should be working...I warn you, Joseph Buquet that I will finally...finally give you exactly what I owe you, and nothing less. By my hands, you will get what you deserve."

I did not stay to see his reaction to my words. However, over the past week, I saw very clearly that he did not heed my warnings. He was just as careless and clumsy as always, and his eyes and hands were always where they did not belong.

I had not planned on carrying out my end of the deal tonight. I would never have done what I did with so many young girls present. But after I made my little...announcement from the dome, I saw him start to pursue me. I had to do what I had to do, Antoinette, to protect the girls and to save my life. You must believe me on this.

I am telling you this, dear friend, so that you might be comforted. You did not rescue, nor are you aiding, a heartless killer. I gave Joseph Buquet a chance. It was he who was not smart enough to take it. I am well aware that I should have confronted him years ago, at the time of his employment. But the fact is, I could not bring myself to face him again, once I realized who it was. I suppose the thing that changed my mind was the fact that I saw him focusing his gaze on Christine Daae, and I think you are well aware of how I feel towards her.

As with all my longer notes to you, Antoinette, you must not show this to anyone. I do not wish to risk the chance of anyone hearing that the Devil's Child still lives inside the opera house, and that you were the one who hid me here. These words are for your comfort only. May they help you sleep far better than I know I will sleep.

Your Friend,

Erik.

Story Three: Weeping Willow

A/N: This story was inspired by a single mental image that's stuck with me ever since I pictured it. Weeping willows have been my favorite tree ever since I can remember. I just like the idea of the branches hanging down like a curtain...a perfect hideaway to read or relax or just...be.

Anyway, before my AN gets more descriptive than the actual story, I just have one more thing to say. I do not own 'Phantom of the Opera' or any of its characters.

"Marguerite, you're still here," I remember saying to you. You were on your dorm room bed, dressed all in black. Even your pale skin and golden hair were caked with ashes and soot. "The fire was weeks ago. I would have thought everyone would be long gone by now." Yes, in the weeks that followed the fire, I had stayed in my caverns, crying all the tears I had for the love I had lost. I was no longer the Phantom of the Opera. I destroyed my masks, smashing them all against the stone cavern walls. I couldn't destroy her, though. I probably never will. She is still precious to me, even though she's a world away, wrapped in the arms of someone else. In those weeks following her departure, I forced myself to build up a different sort of mask. It was a mask of indifference. I did not trust myself to feel any other way. If I had, it would have killed me. And so I left my caverns to explore the home I had destroyed. That's when I found you, and my new mask nearly melted away.

    You turned to face me then. Tears had formed a path down your cheeks through the soot, your brown eyes were surrounded with red, and your hair was all in tangles. You did not show fear. Perhaps your grief had made you numb. Perhaps, like your mother, you allowed your compassion to overshadow any fear you might have had. Either way, you looked at me that day as if I was any normal person. You ran over to me, wrapping your thin arms around me and sobbing into my shirt. "She's gone, Monsieur! Mama is gone...I have nowhere to go now!" Gone? Antoinette Giry...gone? My heart sank at the thought. She had not survived the fire that I had started. I killed her. I killed your mother, and yet here you were, clinging to me with every ounce of strength you had left.

    We stood there for hours it seems, weeping for the woman who had given all of herself to protect and care for us. I imagined her fighting her way through the flames, crying out your name with every last breath. She never found you. You were in my caverns that night. I watched you from behind the curtain, curiosity drying my tears for only a moment. You found my mask, turning it over in your hands. When the mob closed in around you, you persuaded them to go back, to remember the fire. In their fear, they neglected to look back, to see if you were following them. Instead, you fell asleep on my bed, clutching the mask to your heart.

I didn't disturb you, even if I'd had the strength. Instead, I lost myself in my heartbreak, barely noticing when you left. And now, now it seemed that we were both alone. I owed it to your mother to take care of you. She had helped me when I was a boy, hiding me in the caves beneath the opera house. Yes, I would do this for her and for her memory. And so, when your sobs took the rest of your strength, when you passed out in my arms, I carried you down to the shelter of my caverns. I carried you into the lake, holding you in one arm while rubbing the cool water over your fragile and ash-covered body. And oh, if only you could have seen the beauty that was revealed! If only you could have seen yourself through my eyes then. To be sure, you were not like Christine. No, you had beauty that was all your own.

When the water had done it's work, I carried you to my bed, wrapping blankets around you. Cold and soaked as you were, I knew your mother would not have approved of me doing anything with your dress. Instead, I left you to your sleep, hoping that yours was not as filled with nightmares as mine have always been.

I was not used to having company. Especially for an indefinite amount of time. All my life, it had just been me. But I could not throw you out into the streets of Paris to fend for yourself. I could never allow you to face the rejection and loneliness that I had learned to cope with. No, for once in my life, I decided to do something right. My selfishness had led only to heartbreak and destruction. The Phantom was gone; in his place stood a new man. To be sure, I was still broken. But you needed me to be strong. If we were going to survive, I had to place my own desires aside.

While you slept, I built. I carved you a comb out of a piece of wood smoothed by the lake water. I swam to the far side of the lake to fetch the boat Christine and Raoul had taken. Dragging it out of the water, I made it into a bed for you. It was much smaller than my own in comparison, but it was a start. When all that was done, you were still sleeping, and so I prepared some food for you. I did not have much, but I would not let you starve on my watch. And so I sang to you until you woke up. You were still weak, and so I helped you sit so you could eat. I let you lean on me while I moved the comb through your tangles, and when your hair was smooth once more, I tied a black ribbon in your hair. I would have showed you your bed then, but you had already fallen back to sleep.

This time while you slept, I made some of my old clothes into new dresses for you. I remember your face when you saw the dress I made out of my Red Death costume. (I believe it quickly became your favorite, did it not?) I could do nothing about shoes, but with a few scraps of satin I was at least able to make you a pair of ballet slippers. I have always been pleased with your dancing ability. It was the one thing I had never trained myself to do, and so I could appreciate every leap and twirl that you made.

With each project I did for you, I found that it helped to take my mind off of Christine. Still, every once in awhile, she would appear in my thoughts and dreams, and I would find myself gasping for breath, my face covered in sweat and tears, and my chest feeling as though it would burst. In those moments, I would grab for the nearest instrument and begin playing whatever music came to me. While it did not take the pain completely away, it helped me move past my tears and focus on taking care of you.

As the years passed, as you regained your strength to face each day, we helped each other through our grief. Many nights, when I allowed myself to sleep, thoughts and dreams of Christine would force me into a fit of sobs, and you would soon be at my side, caressing my face and assuring me that everything would be okay. Many nights, when I watched you sleep, I could tell when you were thinking about your mother, and I would take you in my arms and let you rest your head on my shoulder.

During the day, while I was busy with my music or some other project, you would lose yourself in one of my many books. You would read about the same foreign lands that I had once read and dreamed about, and we would talk about them as we ate. I never grew tired of the way your eyes lit up, and even when I was in a bitter mood after thinking about Christine, I could never be angry with you for long. To see you cry always broke my heart; I hated to be the cause of it when I did allow my words to go too far. And when you did cry because of me, your face would always light right back up again at the simplest token of my apology. It might have been a white rose(red would always be reserved for Christine...the two of you were so different that even if I had wanted to, I would never have been able to replace her with you.) or a simple sketch or even a new hair ribbon...it didn't matter to you. You once told me that as long as I meant it from the heart, that was all that counted.

Some of your pain, however, I could not ease because it was so deep inside you. You didn't have to tell me or shed any tears. I could see it in your face or hear it in a distant sigh at the dinner table. Even though I was there, sharing in your loneliness, you were still lonely. I could not fully understand, as I had been without my mother all my life. For you, this was completely new, no matter how many years went by. She had kept you close to her side, protecting you from me and from any other dangers lurking in the opera house corridors after curfew. Even though I was lonely for Christine, I could at least remember a time before she set foot inside the opera house.

And then I realized that your pain was worse than my own. Not only had you lost your mother, you had lost a friend close enough to be your sister. I remember asking you why you hadn't gone with Christine. You said that by the time you emerged from the caverns, she and the Vicomte were long gone, giving you up for dead. You said you had no way of getting in touch with them, and you felt it was better this way. "It's best she get a fresh start, with no links to the opera house to fill her with sorrow," you concluded. Though it pained me to hear that, I knew it was true.

My pain, I was used to. I could always turn to my music. I think you would have danced to ease your pain, had there been sufficient room in the caverns. I remember the few times you did attempt to dance, but your movements were more guarded and not as free as we both would have liked. The one time you tried a leap, you nearly ended up in the lake! I would have laughed then, but your face showed so much frustration, I used my effort to reassure you instead.

One thing I knew for sure was that you needed a way to release all your pent up emotions. And so, I gave you free choice of any of my instruments. I would teach you how to play whichever you chose. I remember you selected the harp right away. It was not one of the main instruments that I played, so I was happy to give it to you. You were such a dedicated student, it was not long before I could relax and watch your fingers dance across the strings. I loved watching your eyes close, for I knew exactly what you were feeling. You drank in the music, letting it break through the walls that had built up inside you.

I am mentioning all of this, my dear, because I am trying to remember when it happened. In all the years we spent together in those caverns, I don't remember the exact time that I realized I had fallen in love with you. Was it in a particular smile or a night I watched you sleeping peacefully? Perhaps in a song I heard you play on your harp or in one of the moments you held me while I cried. Maybe it was all of those things. Either way, I remember the first time we kissed. It was a night I had slipped into sleep, and as always, I awoke to find myself drowning in my tears. You were soon at my side, as you had always been in those moments. Unlike all those other times, however, the dream was completely different. Instead of imagining Christine with me, I pictured her with the Vicomte, surrounded by their children. And she was smiling. I did not feel angry or jealous, however. I had watched them dancing in a field, laughing together, and I was completely at peace. She was happy. Hadn't that been what I had always wanted for her? To be sure, it was not with me, but I could never have offered her what she'd really wanted. I knew that now. And so, when you were sitting there, caressing my face, I wanted to show you that things were different. And so, my lips found yours. You were startled at first, but soon I could tell that you were returning my love. Hadn't that been what I'd always wanted?

    The one thing I regret, Marguerite, about all those years we had together is that you were taken from the light and the fresh air above the caverns. I could not give you a proper wedding ceremony as I am sure you had always dreamed about. I could only give you myself. I am sure your mother would have frowned upon the nights we spent wrapped around each other, becoming one as we shared in the passion of our love, but it could not be helped. You told me time and time again that you understood. Even so, there were countless mornings when we were too lazy to get out of bed, when you dozed while I held you close, where I would silently vow to give you something more. You deserved a song.

It's been two years since your death, my dearest Meg, and I have finally finished your song. It has taken so long because I wanted it to be perfect. I began it even before you became ill. Our child you carried inside you took all your energy. I could not leave your side for a single moment. As the months passed and your belly grew, I could tell that something was wrong. We did all we could, dearest Meg, but despite all our efforts, Little Annabelle was born lifeless, and you soon followed her into death.

For the longest time, I stayed by your still bodies, for once again, I was alone. I remembered your words of comfort, however, and they strengthened me. And so, I was finally able to place you in your red dress inside a simple coffin, our daughter in your arms. I forced myself to anchor the coffin in the bottom of the lake so that you're never too far away. But what helped the most was I still felt you with me. As I sat at the organ, lost for words and notes, I could feel your arms around me. I did not deserve you, dearest Meg. I did nothing to deserve your love. Yet you stayed by my side through everything. You gave me a reason to live again…you completed me. And now that you are gone, I can still hope. You have shown me even a disfigured creature can love and be loved in return. I do not picture myself with anyone else, but I don't plan on wallowing in my grief forever either. I will keep writing music that I've always wanted the world to hear. Someday, I will leave the caverns to deliver it, but I will return to you, my love.

It's been two years, and your song is finally perfect. Here it is, my love. Wherever you are, I hope you can see it and know that your love has given me strength to face whatever future lies before me.

Weeping willow

Rise from the ashes

Of all that is past

Weeping willow

Our play is not over

You're still in the cast

You are still here

You can still give

Give shade from the burning sun

And shelter from the pouring rain

Let songbirds build nests in your branches

Let me hide behind your veil of tears

Do not be afraid to weep, dearest willow.

Weeping willow

Rise from the ashes

Of all that is past

Weeping willow

Our play is not over

You're still in the cast

You are still here

You can still give

Your weeping is like a cooling breeze

Filling my ears and my soul with peace

As I am sure it is soothing for you

Take the weight of the world off your shoulders

Do not be afraid to weep, dearest willow

Weeping willow

Rise from the ashes

Of all that is past

Weeping willow

Our play is not over

You're still in the cast

You are still here

You can still give

Dig your roots into the water's edge

As you drink in, let your tears pour out

As you drink, you'll grow deeper

As you weep, you'll grow taller

As you grow, you'll get stronger each day

Weeping willow

Rise from the ashes

Of all that is past

Weeping willow

Our play is not over

You're still in the cast

You are still here

You can still give

Weeping willow,

Rise from the ashes

Weeping willow

You are still here

Weep, willow, weep.

A/N: "Weeping Willow" is my own song, written especially for this story.

I also want to add that one of the strongest bits of feedback I received when I first wrote this story was complaints that I had Meg passing away far too soon. To this, I respond that I agree. Far too many times in real life have people died too young. It's nothing anyone really wants. But it happens, and it was that realism I wanted to convey.

If it be any comfort, I wrote this with it in mind that there were at least five years of them being 'just friends', and at least ten or fifteen years between the first kiss and her final breath.

If this still doesn't comfort you, please...Read on....

Story Four: Winter Rain

Erik stared out the attic window, feeling every drop of frozen rain as if there were no glass between him and the outside. He shivered as he looked at the snow far below him, but the cold he felt, he was sure it was from within his own shattered heart.

Christine. Her name might just as well have been written on every inch of wall space around him. A drop of water landed on his cheek, and he studied the glass to look for any sign of breakage. No, the glass was whole, and he brushed the tear away. *I can't go on like this. Antoinette, why did you not just leave me to my death?* Instead, his old friend had brought him here, to the cottage in the wood once belonging to her late husband's family. She meant to hide him from the bloodthirsty mob...to keep him out of prison. Yet he felt a prisoner anyway. He always had. And the cold January air only emphasized that feeling, as he could not escape.

Or could he? For a brief moment, he toyed with the idea. What would he be risking? His life? *What worth was that to anyone?* But no...Antoinette Giry had gone through far too much trouble and risk for him to do that to her. So he would stay and humor her. That did not mean he had to enjoy it.

"Erik? Are you up there?" *Speaking of...* Erik managed a smirk. He kept silent. *You may take the*

Phantom out of the Opera, but you cannot take the Phantom out of me.... "Erik! You cannot hide for long. This house is much smaller than the Opera Populaire..." *I can adapt....* Her footsteps were on the stairs now. Erik glanced around, deciding on the chimney. Silent as a whisper, he ducked behind the stack of bricks, a smirk now permanent on his face. "Erik..." He jumped as her voice sounded right beside him. *Curses...*

"Antoinette, you're no fun anymore." He sighed and turned to face her.

"Are you coming down for lunch?"

"That is not the proper question, as we both know the answer to that one. Because if you were to ask if I want to go down to lunch, my answer would be a 'no'. But eventually you would convince me to go down anyway. Correct?"

"That is a yes then?" She met his smirk evenly, but for once Erik sensed the faintest trace of a smirk of her own itching to appear. But just as he could not stop being the Opera Ghost, Antoinette could not stop being the no-nonsense ballet mistress. He studied her for a while before letting out a sigh and nodding. She nodded back and led him down the two flights of stairs to the kitchen, where Meg was setting the table. As she finished, she looked up at him with a careful smile. He managed a small smile back before taking a seat farthest from the door. Immediately the little ballerina set a full plate of food down in front of him, and he was almost tempted to glare at her. Almost. He knew it was useless to argue, as the countless arguments on this very subject they'd had before this had revealed that she had inherited her mother's stubbornness. He could almost recite the entire argument by now.

"It's too much."

"Nonsense. It's the perfect amount for you."

"I'm not hungry."

"I'll not have you waste it."

"Well that is your own fault, Little Giry, for giving me all this without asking."

"Don't call me that. And you cannot fault me for caring." At that point, Antoinette would look at him with such an expression that clearly stated:

"Eat or feel my cane across your head." He would then look back at her, wide-eyed, as if to say:

"Antoinette, you wouldn't dare! After all, you were the one who rescued me from the beatings!"

"Then don't test me." Her raised eyebrow would reply. Grumbling under his breath, he would reluctantly shove a forkful of food into his mouth.

This act of defiance would last about halfway through the meal, until Antoinette's face would speak to him once again. "Very well. We understand. You're not happy. But do not cause my daughter to regret her hard work with the cooking." Erik would then sigh and finish every bite quietly. He would then thank Meg with a nod and polite smile, and then he would return to the solitude of the attic.

"Erik?" The former Phantom found himself jumping for the second time within the past hour. True, he had been here for a year now, but he was still unused to hearing the ballerina call him by name.

"Yes, Marguerite?" His voice was filled with impatience and annoyance at being taken by surprise.

"Mama and I have a surprise for you." *More? Have I not been surprised enough today?*

"Oh? I suppose you have figured out how to cause my chair to fall through the floor?"

"Why on earth would we do that?" She raised her eyebrow in such a familiar way that he almost called her Antoinette. He cleared his throat.

"Never mind. What is this surprise?" A bright grin spread across the girl's face then, and she skipped over to the cupboard. Erik turned to throw a questioning glance at Antoinette, but she was merely smiling. *Uh oh.* To his knowledge, Antoinette never smiled...unless she was about to deliver bad news in the kindest way possible, or she would smile when she knew a secret and was not about to tell you. Mostly those smiles were reserved for the secret of him.

She most certainly never smiled at him, which was why he was so nervous now. Before he could open his mouth to speak, a cake was set down in front of him. He quickly looked up at Meg. "Happy Birthday, Erik!"

"Wha--?" He glanced between both Giry women, then back at the cake.

"It was Meg's idea, Erik. She asked me when I told her your story if I knew when your birthday was. As I did not, we decided to celebrate it on the one-year anniversary of you coming here."

"I have never celebrated the day I was born!" Erik was still wide-eyed, but his voice was a bitter growl.

"That's exactly why you deserve this, Erik!" Once again, Meg's cheerfulness melted away his bitterness, and he sighed.

"Very well...thank you..." he mumbled. She then brought two wrapped parcels out from under the table. Giggling, she handed him the first one.

"This one's from me..." Still astonished, Erik slowly and carefully removed the brown paper. Inside a white box, he found a dark crimson scarf, and he slowly lifted it out.

"Marguerite, did you make this?"

"I did..." her voice was suddenly quiet, and he looked at her. Her mouth was formed into a tight smile, as if she were holding something back. He decided not to question it, however. Knowing Meg, she would say it sooner or later.

"Thank you, Marguerite. It's quite lovely." His voice was equally quiet, and his eyes were sincere.

"That second package is from me, Erik..." Antoinette's voice broke through the sudden tension, and Erik slowly reached for it. Inside, he found a pair of metal blades with leather straps attached to them.

"What are they?" He looked at her.

"They're ice skates...they were my husband's..."

"Perhaps when the rain stops, we could go out to the pond and I could teach you..." Meg spoke up, her eyes wide.

"Outside? In this cold?"

"Oh, it's fun, Erik! You'll see..."

"Perhaps." The single word came out in a tone much colder than he'd meant it, but he was just as stubborn as they were, and he would not take it back. Instead, he thanked Antoinette for her gift in a mumbled voice, and the cake was eaten in silence.

Erik spent the remainder of the day in the attic. For once, Antoinette was unable to persuade him to come to supper. No matter how much his stomach growled, he could not bring himself to face their looks of concern, nor could he subject himself to Antoinette's inevitable guilt trip. He was not about to apologize. He had only answered honestly. *No...honesty would have been a flat-out 'no'.* He was cold enough inside without having to expose his skin to the winter chill.

You have that scarf.

I didn't ask for it.

That's not my point. It's there.

And to wear it would only make Marguerite assume that I enjoyed that celebration.

Oh get over it. It was an act of kindness. Accept it.

Why?

Accept it. Erik sighed as he realized he was losing this argument. A scraping sound of metal below broke through his thoughts. He turned back to the window and looked out. The freezing rain had turned to snow right before supper, and it had stopped completely at sunset. The sky was clear now, the moon shining down and reflecting off of the freshly fallen snow. Through the trees, his eyes fell on the pond, now frozen solid, from which he had heard the scraping sound. A lone figure danced upon the ice, spinning and jumping gracefully. He knew those movements.

Marguerite. Yes, it could only be her. And for the first time, he found himself pondering her. She was only months younger than Christine, but admittedly, her dancing ability surpassed that of his pupil. However, aside from watching her perform or keeping a protective eye on her as he did for all the other girls, he had really paid her no mind at all.

Until now. He was not attracted to her, mind you. Only curious. Curious as to why she had had no suitors. Almost as quickly as the question formed in his mind, the answer came to him, and it was so obvious he almost laughed at himself. Potential suitors would have been deathly afraid of Madame Giry! They were so similar and rarely separated that one could not look at the daughter without immediately thinking about the mother.

But was Meg aware of this? Or if she was, did she really mind it? She had always seemed so cheerful and carefree, a trait that worked its way into her every dance routine, making it her signature. But what if that trait was merely a mask, similar to the one he wore?

He watched her skate across the ice, the moonlight the only source by which he could see her. She moved as if she were back on the stage, instead of out in the cold. But he still could not see her face. With a frustrated sigh, he stood up, knowing what he must do.

Meg Giry stopped to rest. It was still early in the night, and she wasn't nearly close to being tired. She shivered now, though ,as if the cold had been chasing her around the pond and had just now caught up to her. She looked up toward the attic window, then sighed. Even if he were up there, she wouldn't see him. He was accustomed to the dark and so he did not use any source of light unless he was working.

She turned away, fighting back the tears that had threatened to fall ever since lunch. He wasn't coming. Why would he? Certainly not for her. Blowing on her hands, she skated forward in an aimless beginning of a routine.

The evening's silence was broken by clumsy footsteps through the snow, accompanied by mumbled cursing. She whirled around, and if she weren't so surprised, she might have laughed at the comical picture before her. There was Erik, former Phantom, hugging a nearby tree with his legs sprawled out in front of him, struggling to keep from completely falling into the snow. He glared up at her. "How on earth do you expect me to walk in these things?" She looked down and allowed a giggle to escape.

"Oh, Erik, you could have waited to put the skates on until you got to the pond!"

" Well this is a bloody fine time to tell me that!" He growled, pulling himself back up to his feet. Stubbornly, he stomped through the snow the rest of the way to the ice, and Meg offered a hand to him. He tilted his head upward, sniffing. "I can manage." Meg nodded doubtfully and moved out of his way. He took a small step onto the ice, and almost immediately, he was doing a full split between the pond and snowy bank. While he was yelping in pain, Meg went over to him and helped him back up. He glared down at her as if she were to blame.

"Will you accept my help now?" In response to her smirk, he placed the other foot onto the ice and inched forward past her. THUD! She didn't have to turn around to know what had happened, but she looked anyway. Yes, there he was, having landed hard on his tailbone. She bent down and offered her hand again. "Now?"

"I don't need your help!"

"Right. I'll remember that when you fall flat on your face."

"Fine. But tell no one. Am I clear?"

"Clear as ice..." she snickered. He glared even harder, causing her to giggle.

"I'm sorry...I couldn't help myself!" He took her hand, muttering, and she lifted him to his feet. As his skates started moving again, he clung to her hand tightly.

"Why am I here again?"

"Because you deserve to experience fun for a change."

"Oh yes. I'm having loads of fun thus far!" His voice dripped with thick, bitter sarcasm.

"It will get better with practice, Erik. Trust me."

As the little dancer looked into his eyes, he felt his heart soften. He nodded slowly and allowed her to grasp his other hand. Pulling him toward the center, she held his gaze so strongly that he felt as if he were floating on air. He allowed her to guide him around the pond, first with both hands, then with one. Slowly, she let go of his hands completely, and he felt his legs begin to wobble all over again. "Keep moving forward, Erik!" She instructed, and he pushed one foot forward, then the other. *Well I'm still on my feet so far...* He repeated the action with a little more confidence, and then again with even more. *This isn't so bad...* "You're doing wonderfully, Erik! Now see if you can catch me!" *She's bloody mad!* Erik threw her a bewildered glare. *There's absolutely no way that I----am going to be beaten by a tiny ballerina of a girl....* Sighing, he relented to his smirk, his Phantom side showing once again.

The moonlight offered no nearby shadows to hide in, but he didn't need them. Little Giry sped across the ice away from him, giggling, and Erik immediately picked up his pace. Within seconds, he was right behind her. *This is too easy.* He pulled back only slightly, watching her. Guessing where she was going, he cut across. Sure enough, she skated right into him, and he caught her shoulders while she shrieked. He let a smirk linger on his face while he inwardly struggled with a very new question. *Now what?* He suddenly realized that he had never been this close to her. He found himself studying her features. Locks of her golden hair peeked out from under her hat, blowing ever so slightly in the almost non-existent breeze. Her cheeks were a deep red, whether from the cold or the rush of the chase, he couldn't be sure. Her mouth was still turned up into a laugh, but it was a laugh slowly fading. He studied her eyes then...her big, brown eyes that were now staring into his. He could see now the unshed tears, hidden behind a thin layer of happiness. He knew it would be a sin to say anything, however. This was her mask...and hers to remove when she was ready. He cleared his throat instead, stepping back and releasing her. "This scarf...it's very warm."

"I'm glad it serves its purpose..." he sensed her confusion growing as she spoke quietly, but there was no going back now to the previous moment.

"You must have worked on it a long time."

"Yes...a little bit each day for almost the entire year we've been here."

"That long?" his eyes widened. "So you had always planned on giving me this?"

"Yes...from the first time I heard your cries in the night...I...I just knew you deserved...something..."

"But why a scarf?" As he asked this, her already deep red cheeks grew redder.

"You'll laugh..."

"I will not." He placed a gloved hand under her chin, forcing her to look back at him.

"I chose a scarf so that...wherever you went...you...would always feel something warm around your neck...almost like...a hug..."

"You...wanted to give me a hug?"

"I told you it was silly."

"Am I laughing, Marguerite?" She slowly shook her head, sighing. "Marguerite, I don't find that silly at all. In fact, a simple hug would have been just as welcome. Yours was the first gift I've ever received in my entire life..." He was crying now, and he brushed at his tears, silently cursing them. He took a deep breath before continuing. "Marguerite...don't you understand? No one...no one has ever thought of me with enough fondness as to give me a gift such as you did today. It's never silly to give from your heart."

As he spoke tearfully, Meg found herself releasing her own tears...tears kept locked away for so long. She stepped into his arms, throwing her arms around him in a tight hug. They shook together then, letting their tears run their course. They did not ask, nor did they explain their reasons for each tear. They just knew...they automatically knew that the hug symbolized the end to their loneliness. If only in friendship, they had each other. And that was enough.

"Meg! Erik! Come inside...I have hot chocolate ready for you!" Madame Giry called, and the two slowly made their way off the ice and through the snow toward the cottage. And once or twice, the air around them heard the sound of muffled thuds and laughter before they picked themselves up and continued on their journey.

Made in the USA
Monee, IL
16 November 2025

35020723R00132